HATCHET:
THE CALL

Gary Paulsen

MACMILLAN
CHILDREN'S BOOKS

First published in Great Britain 1999 by Macmillan Children's Books

This edition published 1999 by Macmillan Children's Books
a division of Macmillan Publishers Limited
25 Eccleston Place, London SW1W 9NF
Basingstoke and Oxford
www.macmillan.co.uk

Associated companies throughout the world

ISBN 0 330 37602 0

1 3 5 7 9 8 6 4 2

A CIP catalogue record for this book is available from
the British Library.

Typeset by SX Composing DTP, Rayleigh, Essex
Printed and bound in Great Britain by Mackays of Chatham plc, Kent

*This book is dedicated to Alana
for taking good care of Linda*

A NOTE ABOUT CHRONOLOGY

Brian was born with *Hatchet* – almost literally. Many readers view him as a nearly real person, someone they wish to know more about, and as a friend. I feel the same way. In answer to requests for more of Brian I have done *The Return* and *Winter* – a sequel and an alternate sequel – and this third novel of his return is, again, a response to readers who want to know what happened to Brian later, after he finally came home.

ONE

Brian sat quietly, taken by a peace he had not known for a long time, and let the canoe drift forward along the lily pads. To his right was the shoreline of a small lake he had flown into an hour earlier. Around him was the lake itself, an almost circular body of water of approximately eighty acres surrounded by northern forest – pine, spruce, poplar and birch – and thick brush.

It was late spring – June 3, to be exact – and the lake was teeming, crawling, buzzing and flying with life. Mosquitos and flies filled the air, swarming on him, and he smiled now, remembering his first horror at the small blood drinkers. In the middle of the canoe he had an old coffee can with some kindling inside it, and a bit of birchbark, and he lit them and dropped a handful of green poplar leaves on the tiny fire. Soon smoke billowed out and drifted back and forth across the canoe and the insects left him. He had repellant with him this time – along with nearly two hundred pounds of other gear – but he hated the smell of it and found it didn't work as well as a touch of smoke now and then. The black-flies and deerflies and horseflies ignored repellant completely – he swore they seemed to lick it off – but they hated the smoke and stayed well off the canoe.

The relief gave him time to see the rest of the activity on the lake. He remained still, watching, listening.

To his left rear he heard a beaver slap the water with its tail and dive – a warning at the intruder, at the strange smoking log holding the person. Brian smiled. He had come to know beaver for what they truly were – engineers, family-oriented home builders. He'd read that most of the cities in Europe were founded by beaver. That beaver had first felled the trees along the rivers and dammed them up. The rising water killed more trees and when the food was gone and the beaver had no more bark to chew they left. The dams eventually broke apart, and the water drained and left large clearings along the rivers where the beaver had cut down all the trees. Early man came along and started cities where the clearings lay. Cities like London and Paris were founded and settled first by beaver.

In front and to the right he heard the heavier footsteps of a deer moving through the hazel brush. Probably a buck because he heard no smaller foot-steps of a fawn. A buck with its antlers in velvet, more than likely, moving away from the smell of smoke from the canoe.

A frog jumped from a lily pad six feet away and had barely entered the water when a northern pike took it with a slashing strike that tore the surface of the lake and flipped lily pads over to show their pale undersides.

Somewhere a hawk *screeeeeennn*ed, and he looked for it but could not see it through the leaves of the trees around the lake. It would be hunting. Bringing home mice for a nest full of young. Looking for something to kill.

No, Brian thought – not in that way. The hawk did not hunt to kill. It hunted to eat. Of course it had to kill to eat – along with all other carnivorous animals – but the killing was the means to bring food, not the end. Only man hunted for sport, or for trophies.

It is the same with me as with the hawk, Brian felt. He turned the paddle edgeways, eased it forward silently and pulled back with an even stroke. I will kill to eat, or to defend myself. But for no other reason.

In the past two years, except for the time with Derek on the river, in a kind of lonely agony he had tried to find things to read or watch that brought the woods to him. He missed the forest, the lakes, the wild as he thought of it, so much that at times he could not bear it. The guns-and-hunting magazines, the hunting and fishing videos on television sickened him. Men using high-velocity weapons to shoot deer or elk from so far away they could barely see them, or worse, blasting them from a blind or the back of a Jeep; baiting bear with pits full of rotten meat and shooting them with rifles that could stop a car; taking bass for sport or money in huge contests with fancy boats and electronic gear that located each fish individually.

Sport, they called it. But they weren't hunting or fishing because they needed to; they were killing to kill, not eat, to prove some kind of worth, and he stopped reading the magazines and watching the videos. His survival in the wilderness had made him famous, in a small way, and some of the magazines interviewed him, as did some of the hunting and sporting shows on television, but they got it all wrong. Completely wrong.

"Boy conquers savage wilderness!" some magazines said in the blurbs on the covers. "Learns to beat nature . . ."

It wasn't that way. Had never been that way. Brian hadn't conquered anything. Nature had whipped him, not the other way around; had beaten him down and pounded the stupidity out of his brain until he had been forced to bend, forced to give, forced to learn to survive. He had learned the most important fact of all, and the one that is so hard for many to understand or believe: Man proposes, nature disposes. He hadn't conquered nature at all – he had become part of it. And it had become part of him, maybe *all* of him.

And that, he thought as the canoe slid gently forward, had been *exactly* the problem.

TWO

If he had to name the final straw that had done it, that had driven him away, driven him back, it would, he thought, have had to be the noise . . .

Another stroke of the paddle and the canoe slithered along the water. It was a beautiful canoe, named *The Raft* – made of Kevlar, sixteen feet long and weighing only fifty-two pounds empty, as smooth as fish skin. It seemed to fit nature as well as wind or water, seemed almost alive.

He had tried. He had tried as hard as he could to fit in, to become normal again. After the fame wore off, the novelty of telling people what had happened, showing them how he'd made the first fire, how to make a bow, how to hunt – when all that was done and the world around him had returned to a semblance of normalcy – he'd tried to fit back in. For a year and more he had acted – in his mind anyway – as if he were normal.

School. He'd gone back to school and tried to become reacquainted with old friends. They were still friends, glad to welcome him back into their company. The problem wasn't them, it was him.

"Let's go down to the mall and play some video games," they would say. Or play softball, or ride bicycles or, or, or. And he would try. But sports and shooting electronic bullets or rays at imaginary enemies that clomped across screens seemed silly, pale in comparison to what his real life had been like: having moose attack him, living on the edge of starving, living only because his thinking, his brain, kept him alive. He couldn't get into the games, couldn't believe in them. It was the same with the people who made up extreme sports just to prove they could do it. Rock climbers, "radical" skate-boarders, wilderness programs that were supposed to toughen up city kids – rich kids – and make them better people. All games.

He drifted away. Talking about which girl liked which boy or who was cool and who was not or who would be at what party or who was or who was not doing drugs – all of it became a swirl around him. He heard the sounds, nodded, tried to appear interested, but in the end, sitting alone in his room one evening, he realized that he couldn't care less about any of it.

He sought solitude. Even when he was in a group, nodding and smiling and talking, he was alone in his mind. Sometimes his thinking would catch up with the reality of what was happening and he

7

would see himself talking as if in the third person. Here is Brian, he would think, telling Bill that he can't go to the movie tonight because . . .

Reality began to slip away from him. Not that he was mentally different, or mentally ill, so much as that it just bored him. There was a small park in town, a stand of trees with some hedges, and he found himself going there more and more, walking past the park on his way home from school, stopping under the trees, closing his eyes, remembering the woods, the wind, the movement of leaves, the world without the incessant noise.

Not just cars and horns and sirens and television, which he had come to hate because it took so much away from his thinking, but people talking and planes flying over, doors slamming – it all rolled into one kind of static sound, one noise.

It came to a head in of all places the front entryway of Mackey's Pizza Den. Brian had become aloof, sometimes unaware of the social life around him, and without knowing it had upset a boy named Carl Lammers. Carl was a football player, a large boy – his nickname was Hulk – and also a bully who envied Brian's celebrity. Brian didn't know him. Apparently Carl thought Brian had said something bad about him and he was coming out of Mackey's Pizza Den just as Brian was walking in with a boy and girl from school. The boy was small and thin – he was named Haley – and the girl was named Susan and she thought Brian was great and wanted to know him better and had invited him for a pizza so she could talk to him. Haley had been standing nearby and thought the invitation included him, to Susan's disappointment.

Carl had asked Susan on a date once and she had refused him. Seeing her with Brian made his anger that much worse.

He saw Brian through the glass of the door, saw him walking with Susan, and Carl threw his whole weight into his shoulder and slammed the door open, trying to knock Brian off balance.

It all went wrong. Brian was too far to the side and the door missed him. It caught Haley full on, smashing his nose – blood poured out immediately – and slammed him back into Susan. The two of them went flying backward and Susan fell to the ground beneath Haley and twisted her kneecap.

"Oh . . ." she moaned.

For a moment everything seemed to hang in place. The door was open, Carl standing there and Brian off to the side, his face perplexed – he had been thinking about the woods when it happened – and Susan and Haley on the ground, blood all over Haley's face and Susan moaning, holding her knee.

"What—?" Brian turned back to Carl just as Carl took a swing at his head. Had it connected fully,

Brian thought, it would have torn his head off. Dodging before it caught him, he missed the total force of the blow, but even then it struck his shoulder and knocked him slightly back and down on one knee.

Then things came very quickly. Haley was blinded by the blood in his eyes but Susan saw it all and still didn't believe it.

"Something happened," she said later. "Something happened to Brian – Carl just disappeared . . ."

In that instant Brian totally reverted. He was no longer a boy walking into a pizza parlor. He was Brian back in the woods, Brian with the moose, Brian being attacked – Brian living because he was quick and focused and intense on staying alive – and Carl was the threat, the thing that had to be stopped, attacked.

Destroyed.

Brian came off the ground like a spring. His eyes, his mind, searched for a weapon, something, anything that he could use but there was nothing; pavement, a brick wall, a glass door. Nothing loose. It didn't matter. The thought did not slow his movement, and he had himself. He had his hands.

He did not box. Nothing in nature boxed, hit with closed fists. Instead he kept his hands open and jabbed with the thick heels of his palms, slamming

10

them forward in short blows that taken singly might not have done much damage. But he did not hit once, or twice – he smashed again and again, striking like a snake, the blows multiplying their force.

Carl played football, and physical contact was part of it. He actually enjoyed the shock of blocking, tackling. But this . . . this was insane. He felt as if he were being struck all over at the same time. Brian hit his eyes, slamming them again and again until Carl couldn't see and reeled back against the wall, his hands up to cover his face. He tried to quit.

"All right . . ."

Brian was past hearing Carl. He was past anything. He was in a place where normal rules didn't apply. Carl was temporarily blinded, but he was far from finished in Brian's mind. With Carl's face covered, his stomach was open and Brian struck there, pleased to find he was overweight and soft. A place to aim, a place to hurt. He hit again and again, still using the heels of his hands, his wrists rigid, the blows up and into the top of the stomach, forcing air out of the diaphragm so it whistled from Carl's nostrils.

Carl's hands dropped to cover his stomach and Brian went for his face again, pounded the eyes so they were swollen shut, blow on blow until Carl's hands came up again. When Carl crouched, tried to protect everything and left the back of his head open, Brian took him there, clubbing down with both hands joined, pounding until Carl was on his hands and knees, his nose bleeding, the air wheezing from his lungs.

It can't get up, Brian thought, surprised how cool he was. He wasn't angry. I can't let it get up or it will hurt me, he thought. At first he didn't realize that he was thinking *it* and not *him*. It has to stay down. I have to keep it down.

Carl was on the edge of being senseless but something – perhaps the training of football – would not let him collapse completely. It would have been better if he had. Brian couldn't stop. He kept clubbing down, working silently, crouched on his knees now, bringing his joined hands in a double fist again and again onto the back of Carl's head as if he were cutting wood.

Somebody was screaming and other people were running toward them, clawing at Brian, pulling him up and away, but he kept working at it, centered, focused on clubbing Carl down even as they pulled him off. They would pull him away for a moment and he would tear loose and attack again.

"Don't let it up," he said. "I have to keep it *down* . . ."

12

THREE

Police came to the pizza place. They called an ambulance and took Carl to the hospital, where it was found that the skin around his eyes was severely bruised, as were his ribs and his stomach. Though it was not really necessary they kept him in the hospital overnight for observation, which made his condition seem much more severe than it was.

The police handcuffed Brian and put him in the backseat of the car while they interviewed witnesses. Susan came to the car but the police pulled her away.

"No talking," they told her. "No talking to the boy."

"But he didn't do anything wrong. Carl attacked him. Brian was just—"

"No talking to the boy."

In a short time the police came back and removed the handcuffs but they wouldn't let Brian go. Instead they drove him home and he had the unpleasant experience of having police with

13

him when his mother opened the door. She was thin, and dressed for work in her real-estate blazer.

"Brian . . .? What . . ."

"There was a fight at Mackey's Pizza. Your boy was beating up on another boy."

"Brian? Is that true?"

Brian said nothing.

"Brian, is that true?" she repeated. "Were you fighting?"

He looked at his mother. He thought briefly of trying to tell her the truth: that it hadn't been the Brian she knew but a different one, a totally different person; that it hadn't been a fight but an automatic reaction. It hadn't happened because it hadn't been him – it had been some kind of animal. A boy animal. No, an animal-boy. I am animal-boy, he thought, and tried not to smile.

"It is most definitely *not* funny."

He shook his head. "I know. I didn't mean it's funny. I don't know exactly what happened . . ."

"Did you fight? Like the policeman says?"

He thought a moment. "I was . . . reacting. Protecting myself."

"The boy was beaten senseless," the policeman said. "He didn't know his name."

"He attacked me."

"We were told several versions," the policeman

said to Brian's mother. "Apparently they were fighting over a girl."

"A girl?" She looked at Brian. "You have a girl?"

Brian shook his head. "No – it wasn't that way at all. I was coming in the door and he slammed the door open and Susan was knocked down and he hit me and I . . ."

But they didn't hear him. Even if they had listened they wouldn't have heard him, not really. They would never understand him.

So he shrugged and played dumb and let them think what they wanted. It didn't matter because he was starting to understand it now, was starting to see what had to happen, what he needed to do.

I know someone, a counselor," the policeman said. "He's a retired cop and works with boys. I'll give you his name." The policeman took out a notebook and wrote a name and number on a page, tore it out and gave it to Brian's mother. "Here. Call him and he can talk to your boy . . ."

Animal-boy, thought Brian. Not boy, animal-boy. But he didn't smile.

" . . . maybe he can straighten him out."

Not unless he can see into my heart, Brian thought.

FOUR

The sign was hung on the side of an office attached to a house.

CALEB LANCASTER
Family Counseling
Please Come In

It wasn't really an office as much as it was a room stuck on the corner of a two-car garage. It had probably been a workshop, Brian thought. He stopped at the door. This cop retired and is making money on the side by counseling boys in his old workshop. Great. Just great. He'll tell me to get good grades, don't fight, don't do drugs, obey my parents – *and* the police – and send me on my way. After getting a check from Mom, which is really a check from the money I've saved, since Mom doesn't have any money. Great.

He had talked to a counselor briefly the first year after he'd come back but there hadn't really been anything wrong then. He hadn't started to miss the woods as much as he would later – and football

16

players hadn't attacked him yet either, he thought, looking at the sign.

For a moment he played with the idea of turning and leaving. This was so stupid. There was nothing wrong with him. He had come back at somebody who was attacking him. He had come back a little hard, maybe, but just the same . . .

His hand turned the knob without his really meaning it to and the door opened.

"Hello. You must be Brian."

Brian stopped just inside the door and his eyes moved and in two seconds he had taken in everything in the room. Plain white walls, some cheap pictures of woods and mountains that didn't seem to match the rest of the space, a framed document of some kind. The desk was gray-green metal. There was one chair facing the front of the desk – an old iron office chair. Along one wall was a gray-green metal bookcase filled with books so heavy the shelves sagged. The floor was clean gray concrete.

It was maybe the ugliest room he had ever seen.

Behind the desk sat what Brian could only think of as a wall of a man. He wasn't fat, just enormous and richly black, with a smile that grew wider as he stood and held out his hand. Brian almost moved back. This man had to be nearly seven feet tall. He literally almost filled the room.

"I'm Caleb."

Brian took his hand and felt himself being moved toward the chair across from Caleb.

"Take a seat, any seat." He laughed. "As long as it's this one."

Brian sat, waited.

"They tell me you're the boy who lived in the woods. The one who was all over television a couple of years ago."

Brian nodded.

"Is that right?"

Brian nodded again and realized with a start that Caleb was blind. "Yes . . ."

Caleb laughed, deep and booming. "You were nodding."

"Yes. I'm sorry. I didn't know . . ."

"Don't be sorry. It's flattering that you took so long to see it."

"Did it happen when you were a cop?"

Another laugh. "Not really. I got a headache one day, a really fierce one while I was working, and three days later I was blind."

"Just like that?"

"Just like that. The doctors had some fancy names for what happened but I like to keep things simple. I had a headache. I went blind. That's it. But we're not supposed to talk about me. We're supposed to talk about why you beat the hell out of that football player."

Brian leaned back.

"If you want to."

Brian took a breath.

"Or we could talk about something else."

"I didn't beat the hell out of him."

"They took him to the hospital . . ."

"He attacked me."

"Over a girl," Caleb said.

"No. Or maybe. I don't know. He just slammed out the door and hit me."

"And you hit him back."

Brian nodded, then remembered. "Yes."

"Tell me about the woods."

"Pardon?"

"The woods. Tell me about them. I'm a city boy and don't know anything about woods. What are they like?"

"I . . ." Brian shrugged. "They're all right."

"All right? That's all? After all you did that's all you can say? I heard you had to eat bugs and almost died. What was it like – *really* like?"

Brian paused, remembering. A blade of grass that moved, the way a rabbit turned its head just before an arrow hit it, a flash of color when a fish rolled in the water.

"I don't think you would understand. Nobody

19

who hasn't been there can really know . . ."

Caleb nodded and was silent. Then he spoke softly. "Tell me one thing then."

"What do you mean?"

"Tell me one thing, one part of it that I can see in my mind and understand. You can do that, can't you?"

Brian shrugged. "I guess so. Which part do you want to know about?"

"You pick it."

Brian thought for nearly a full minute. Moose attacks, wild wind, good kills, near misses, food – lord, *food* when he was starving – and the fierce joy that came when a hunt worked. All of it was there, every little and big thing that had happened to him in a summer and a winter, and in the end, he decided to tell Caleb about a sunset.

There had been many sunsets and they were all beautiful; every one had had different light, different sounds, and he remembered them all the way somebody who watches a wonderful movie can remember every bit of the movie.

The one he described for Caleb was in the winter. It had been a still, unbelievably cold day when trees exploded and the sky was so brilliantly clear that when he looked into the blue it didn't seem to have a limit, didn't seem to end. It was late afternoon and he had eaten hot food inside his shelter and gone outside to get wood in for the night. The sun was below the tree line but there was still light and the sky was rapidly turning a deep cobalt blue and Brian could see a single bright star – or was it a planet? Venus, perhaps, near where the sun had disappeared.

Suddenly – and it was so quick he almost missed it – a spear of golden light shot from the sun and seemed to pierce the star. Like an arrow of gold light, one brilliant shaft there and gone, and while he watched, transfixed, another shaft came and then another. Three times. Three light-arrows from the sun shot through the star.

It made him believe, made him *know*, that there was something bigger than he was, something bigger than everybody, bigger than all. He thought it must mean something, had to mean something, but he could not think what. Three arrows of light. Three-Arrow. Maybe a name, maybe a direction. Later, after he came back and was trying to understand all that had happened, he read that early Inuits in the North saw the northern lights and believed them to be the souls of dead children dancing. Brian knew it was really the ionosphere ionizing but he still wanted it to be the souls of dead children playing, wanted it to mean more, and it was the same with this sunset.

It was so beautiful it took his breath and he

21

stood, his arms full of wood, staring at the sky until the sun, the star and the light were gone, wanting it all to mean more.

He tried to tell Caleb everything about the sunset every color, every shade, the small sounds of the ice crack-singing on the lake, the hiss of the cold sky, the rustle of powder snow settling.

Told it all and when he was done he looked across the desk and saw that Caleb was crying.

FIVE

"Did I say something wrong?"

Caleb wiped his cheeks with the back of his hand. "No. I was just . . . moved . . . by how it must have looked. It sounds so incredibly beautiful . . ."

"It is. It's . . . It's everything. Just everything."

"And you miss it."

There it was, out in the open. The thought had been in Brian's mind ever since the police had brought him home, and before that without his knowing it. Small at first, then bigger and bigger. And Caleb had seen it.

"Yes. More than anything. I miss . . . being there. I feel I should go back . . ."

"Is it running away or running to?"

Brian frowned, thinking. "It's neither. It's what I am now – for better or worse. It's more that I just can't be with people anymore."

"You hate people?"

"No – not like that. I don't hate them. I have friends and love some people. My mother and father. And I've tried to do things with people and go to school and be . . . normal. But I can't – it just doesn't work. I have been, I have seen too much. They talk about things that don't interest me and when I talk about what I think about, what I see, they just glaze over."

"Like the sunset . . ."

Brian nodded, then remembered again that Caleb couldn't see. But he'd "seen" more of Brian than anybody else. "That and other things, many other things . . ."

"Can you tell me some of the other things?"

"Like the sunset?"

Caleb nodded. "If you wish. Whatever you want to tell me."

Again Brian paused, thinking.

"If it's too private . . ."

"No. It's not that. It's more that what I've seen is different from how people think things really are. Television makes them see things that aren't real, that don't exist. If I tell you how it *really* is you won't believe it."

"Try me."

Brian sighed. "All right. Mice have houses and make towns under the snow in the winter."

"Make towns?"

"See? You don't believe it, do you?"

Caleb shook his head. "I meant that I wanted to know more. Please tell me about it."

And so Brian did. He had been moving around a clearing one day on snowshoes, hunting. It was cold but not the crippling cold that came sometimes and he had an arrow on the bowstring of his war bow just in case, when he looked out in the clearing and saw a fox make a high, bounding jump and bury its head in the snow, its tail sticking up like a bottle brush.

The fox came up with snow all over its face, looked around – Brian froze and the fox didn't see him – then looked down at the snow again. It cocked its head, listening, then made another leap, fully four feet in the air, and dove headfirst into the snow again.

This time it came up with a mouse wriggling in its front teeth. The fox bit down once, killed it, swallowed it and then listened again, bounced in the air again and came up with another.

The fox did it eight more times and got three more mice before trotting out of the clearing and away. Brian watched the whole thing, wondered briefly about eating mice and thought better of it. Not that he was squeamish but he had a deer by this time and plenty of meat and besides, it would take probably thirty or forty mice to make a meal and cleaning them – gutting each mouse and skinning it – would take a lot of work and time.

Still, he was curious. He hadn't thought much

about mice but now that he did he supposed they would be hibernating. But the ones that came up in the fox's mouth were wriggling. Clearly they hadn't been sleeping.

Brian moved into the clearing and stared at the snow, listening as the fox had done, but he couldn't hear anything. He took off his snowshoes and used one of them as a shovel, carefully scooping away the snow until he was down to grass, and it was here he found the truth.

The grass had been tall when winter came. When the snow fell on it the grass bent over on itself and made a thick, thatch-like roof the snow couldn't penetrate. It was beneath this roof that the mice lived.

Brian cleared more of the snow and found small, round tunnels leading from one snug grass room to another, little homes under the snow. In itself the grass would not have been that warm but the snow – two feet of powder over the top – made a wonderful insulator and the rooms were dry and cozy looking. When Brian lay on his stomach and looked down one of the tunnels he saw that light penetrated the snow, and as he watched, a field mouse came around a corner and saw Brian. It froze and turned and ran back. During the ten minutes he watched five more mice came down the tunnel and ran back when they saw it was open.

A whole city was under there, he thought as he watched – a mouse city. There must have been hundreds of mice down in the grass tunnels and rooms, protected and snug for the winter, except that it wasn't completely safe. The fox knew they were down there and with those big ears it listened until it heard one moving through a tunnel. Then it leaped in the air and pounced headfirst, driving down through the snow and grass to catch the mouse.

"The fox didn't hit all the time," Brian told Caleb, finishing the story. There were probably hundreds he missed living down there, so most of the mice were fine. It made me feel foolish, trying to keep my cave warm, working so hard to live. The mice had it all figured—"

"Does anybody else know this?"

"I haven't seen it in books or anywhere. And nobody would believe me if I told them."

"I believe you."

"Well – almost nobody."

"Tell me more."

"About the mice?"

"About the woods. What time is it?"

"Three o'clock."

"Oh. I have another appointment at three-thirty. Why don't you come back tomorrow and talk to me?"

"As a counselor?"

"No – there's nothing wrong with you."

"There isn't?"

"Not a thing. In the attack you were simply defending yourself – the best way you knew how. I just want to hear more about the north woods. You don't have to come if you don't want to – and tell your mother there's no charge. It's just that you make it sound so . . . real. I want to hear more."

"All right." Brian rose. "I'd be glad to come back tomorrow." And he was surprised to find as he walked to the door that he meant it.

SIX

At first, things didn't go nicely and he would look back later and wonder at the timing and the way life worked. It was spring, with two months of school left. School became difficult for Brian – everybody knew about the fight. Some thought he was a hero and some thought he was crazy, and most kept away from him. He ran into Carl Lammers now and then in the hallway and Lammers stayed well clear of him.

Susan decided Brian was just exactly the Right Person in the Whole World for her and made an effort to be near him whenever she could, walk with him whenever she could, talk to him whenever she could. He knew she was a good person, but she was very popular, a member of all the clubs who did all the activities, and she was always trying to draw Brian out, to make him talk about himself. Finally he began to avoid her, in as nice a manner as possible, but word went around that he was stuck-up, and soon Susan and everybody else left him alone.

Though he liked the solitude, oddly it made him

feel bad and made going to classes difficult. He began to hate school and went only because he had to. He studied out of habit, and strangely his grades stayed up. Months later he thought that he would have gone crazy except for Caleb and the dream.

The dream came when he was awake. In school, at home with his mother, whenever there was a moment of quiet or boredom, his thoughts would glaze over and the dream would come.

It was a dream of getting ready. Always that – getting ready. Ready to go back. Ready to go . . . home. To go home to the woods and find . . . he didn't know what. To find himself, something about himself. Often the dream would be about what he would take. The kind of weapon – always a bow, never a gun – the kind of arrows, fishing equipment, clothing. Not just to go back and survive this time, but to live and to be happy where he lived. Just to be. The right kind of equipment. His canoe. A good bow, several dozen good arrows. The right pair of snowshoes. Some hooks and line. A good sleeping bag. Tarp to make a shelter. Maybe a tent. A pot to cook in. No, two pots. One big and one medium. Clothes for fall and winter. Good boots, moccasins.

He worked the list endlessly in his mind, improving it, changing it and, finally, writing it down on the list. He carried it in a notebook wherever he went, making changes as they came to him, meticulously noting each detail of each item.

I have become truly anal, he thought once when he changed the kind of arrowheads from the fancy new razor heads to the old-fashioned MA-3s – three-bladed army-issue arrowheads that needed sharpening but were so strong you could hit a rock without hurting them.

But it was more than just being picky. In the end he was keeping his sanity, arranging his life. At first the List was a guide from the dream to reality but when he had perfected the List he started to gather the items on it, ordering from catalogs in the backs of hunting and fishing magazines. His mother knew he was ordering but she was involved in other things and left him mostly to himself, and as he received items he put them in his room and she didn't question him.

The first thing to come was a bow. He did not want to get too complicated and stayed away from the compound bows with wheels and pulleys. They were more accurate, maybe, and far easier to pull, but he sensed they would break with rough use. Instead he wrote to Blakely, a man who made long-bows and shorter recurved bows and ordered what Blakely called a short longbow. True longbows were fine but very long, as the name implied, and Brian knew that in brush they would hang up on branches and be hard to use. He ordered a shorter version with forty-five-pound pull at twenty-six inches. He hadn't been sure of the pull weight, but he told Blakely his size and what he wanted to use it for – general hunting – and Blakely told him to keep it low. Blakely made bows with up to 120 pounds pull, but they were brutal and, he wrote, "If the arrowhead is sharp it will penetrate from a softer bow as well as a hard one."

The bow was beautiful, a mix of ironwood and rosewood laminated in thin strips with fiberglass on the front and back. Blakely included four extra strings. He also sold arrows so Brian bought a hundred Port Orford cedar shafts and all the tools and precut feathers and nocks he would need to make his own arrows. Blakely also sent along fifty of the MA-3 broadheads and field points for the arrows so he could practice without using the MA-3s. Brian had never made arrows before but there were full instructions with the equipment and Brian found it easy to do. He went to a garden store and brought home three hay bales. He put them up in the backyard and put a cardboard target in front. When he had six arrows finished he started shooting each day.

It was incredible. He was used to weapons he'd made with crude arrows and fire-hardened points, and he was amazed at the difference. The bow was smooth and clean and quiet and the arrows flew with a tight accuracy that at first he couldn't believe. On the first day he had several shots where he actually hit one arrow with another in the center of the cardboard target.

To protect his fingers he used a simple leather tab that Blakely had thrown in and he must have shot two hundred times the first day. He didn't use sights but shot by instinct – let his mind and eye "feel" where the arrow would go as he'd done with his war bow in the woods – and within a week he could consistently hit a six-inch circle in the cardboard from twenty yards.

Just this one part of the List, the bow and arrows, took two and a half weeks, not counting the time for shipping. The work gave him something to do, kept him active.

Along with the List and practice, he had Caleb.

Five days a week he went to Caleb's house after school. His mother thought it was for counseling, though she wondered that no bills came. In a way, it was true. Counseling was a matter of telling somebody something and getting help with a problem, and that was what he was doing with Caleb.

He told Caleb about his life in the woods, and though Caleb seldom said much this talking helped Brian to understand himself and what was happening – and what was going to happen to him.

Caleb would make a pot of tea – nothing fancy,

just hot water and a tea bag with some cream and sugar – and have a cup waiting when Brian got there. Brian had never thought much of tea but the first time he put sugar in it and sipped it while he spoke it somehow seemed to always have been a part of him. It was so natural that after only a small bit of thought he added tea to his list for the woods. Tea – and sugar in cubes.

He would take the tea, sit down in the iron chair, look at Caleb and say. "What do you want to hear about today?"

"I wouldn't even know what to ask. You pick it."

And Brian would think a moment and then tell a story of moose or fishing or the sun on the water or the way beaver build a house or the lonely cry of a loon in the night or the stomach-tightening wail of a wolf singing to the moon and Caleb would listen quietly, his eyes staring off, sometimes crying or laughing, sometimes surprised, sometimes sad.

Then there came a day when school was nearly done, when Brian had received nearly all the things on the List, and Caleb sighed and said, "It's time for you to go back, to find what you're looking for . . ."

Brian agreed. They'd spoken about his going back and how he had to know what it was that pulled him and made him feel empty. "But I don't know exactly how to do it," Brian said.

"I'll help you."

"You will?"

Caleb shrugged. "I'm supposed to be helping you 'recover your mental health,' aren't I? Well, it's clear that for you to be mentally healthy you have to go back to the woods and find what you left there."

"That's true."

"What about that Cree family who rescued you? The trappers?"

"The Smallhorns." Brian thought of them often. "What about them?"

"Didn't they want you to come back and visit them?"

Brian stared. "Of course. It's perfect. Why didn't I think of that?"

SEVEN

It wasn't easy at first. He had expected difficulties with his parents and he wasn't mistaken. His mother had a terrible fear of the bush – which had developed in the weeks when he had disappeared and she had had to believe he was dead. They talked many nights before she relented. He was older now, more seasoned, and she knew that. He had done well the past summer, when he had returned with Derek. With Caleb's help, his mother came around.

"How will you find the Smallhorns?" she asked.

"The pilot, the man who flew me out, will know where they are."

Brian had kept the pilot's name. The man had a one-plane operation working out of International Falls, on the Minnesota-Canada border, and Brian called.

"The Smallhorns? Yeah – they're up in the Williams Lake area in a fish camp but I'm not due to go up there until fall. I'm booked solid all summer with fishing charters. I can't take the time to run you up there."

"How about getting me close? I can make my own way in a canoe."

"Just a minute." Brian heard papers shuffling as the pilot went through his records. "Yeah, here. I'm due to take a couple of guys fishing in ten days. We're going to the Granite Lake area and with my fuel I can take you maybe another hundred miles. That's still a hundred miles short of the Smallhorns' camp but it's all chain lakes up there and you can do it without any really bad portages. I'll give you a good map. How heavy is your gear?"

"Maybe two hundred pounds, plus me and a canoe. Can you haul a canoe?"

"Sure. On the floats. We're taking one canoe and I can fit yours on the other float. When are you figuring on coming out?"

"I'm not . . . sure."

"I'm due to make a supply run to them in the fall before trapping season and bad weather sets in. You could come out then."

"Sure."

"All right – you just fly up to International Falls and I'll meet you there."

He didn't exactly lie to his mother, he just didn't tell her the whole truth. She thought the plane was taking him all the way and he didn't correct her. When he called to tell his father about his "visit", he left the same impression, although he didn't

37

think it would have mattered to his father that he planned to do the last hundred miles by canoe. His relationship with his father had also changed in the last year – they had grown somehow farther apart and closer at the same time. His father no longer seemed to think of him as a boy and didn't talk down to him. Now he spoke to Brian more as an equal.

"It sounds great," he said. "A long visit will do you good. You'll have a wonderful time."

The canoe was the problem. He had to pay extra for shipping it and from Minneapolis north he had to send it by truck. The airlines took care of all the arrangements. He had to send it early for the canoe to be there when he arrived and he worried that something would happen to it – hated to let it out of his sight. But the airline called to say when it arrived safely in International Falls – a full four days before he flew up himself.

The rest of his gear he put in two backpacks, except for the bow and arrows. He checked the bow on the plane in a thick paper tube and the arrows went in boxes with his packs.

He did not take winter or cold-weather gear except for a windbreaker-anorak and two Polar Fleece pullovers. He wasn't sure why. When he walked around the house or through town or was at school there was not a thought in his mind of coming back. Perhaps he would, but . . . As television had soured for him he had started to read more, studied history more and knew that in the past many young men his age, nearly sixteen – were away and into their lives. In the Civil War sixteen-year-olds had been fighting, dying. With his parents' permission, Brian could enlist in the army at seventeen. For better or worse, he was set on his own path and he didn't think of coming back and yet he didn't take winter gear.

It was the lack of room, he told himself – he could get it later. He just didn't have enough room.

The last two weeks were filled with calling the travel agent, assuring everybody he would be all right, making certain everything on the List was packed, and visiting Caleb.

Then finally the last day came and he visited Caleb to say goodbye.

"You'll write," Caleb said, and it was not a question but a statement. "I'll want to know how you're doing."

Brian nodded. "Except that I won't be able to get any mail out."

"In the fall. There will be the supply run you told me about. You could send letters then."

"I will. I promise."

"Well, then . . ."

Brian stood and they started to shake hands.

Then Caleb moved around the desk and grabbed him up in a bear hug. Brian's feet actually left the ground.

"I'll write," he promised when he was loose.

"Tell me everything," Caleb said. "Tell me about light and colors. All of it . . ."

"I will." He paused. "I don't know how to thank you."

Caleb smiled. "You already have. Just write . . ."

His mother drove him to the airport and helped him with all his gear. At the check-in she put her hand on one of the packs and he looked at her and she was crying.

"I'll be fine, Mom."

"I know. I just remembered how it all started. The small plane, and the hatchet I gave you. It all seems so long ago and it was just two years."

No, Brian thought, hugging her. It was more than that. It was a lifetime ago.

"You're grown now. Your father and I were talking about it last week. But when I see you like this, getting ready to leave, I think of you back then when you really *were* a little boy." She took a deep breath. "I don't want you to go."

He didn't say anything because there was nothing to say. She was his mother and he loved her. He loved his father too but he had to do this thing or he would . . . he didn't know what he would do. Go crazy. Never be right. Somehow inside he would die.

"I'll write and send it out by bushplane."

"You'd better."

She stayed with him at the gate, talking of small things and touching him now and again until it was time to board, and then she waved as he walked down the tunnel to the plane.

EIGHT

Brian flew to Minneapolis and changed to a shuttle flight to International Falls. He got in at three in the afternoon and found his canoe and paddles waiting at the airport. He called the bush pilot, who answered on the first ring and told him to get his gear down to the dock by a store in Ranier, a little town on Rainy Lake near International Falls.

Brian took a cab to the dock with all his gear. The driver had rope to tie the canoe to the rack on top of the car, said he did it all the time what with all the people coming to the Boundary Waters Canoe Area. He waited on the end of the dock and in an hour a bushplane with twin floats circled once, landed and idled up to the dock.

"Hi, Brian!" The pilot jumped out and tied the plane to the dock. "Good to see you again. Just put your gear in the backseat and we'll tie your canoe on the float. Won't take a minute."

In five minutes they were taxiing away from the dock. The pilot throttled back and moved down the lake a quarter mile to a small building beside another dock.

"My shack." The pilot pointed with his chin. "I could have had you take the cab there but the cabbies don't like the road. It's two miles through the woods and mostly mud. You got food?"

Brian had been looking at the building. "Pardon?"

"Do you have food with you? Thing is, the two fishermen are coming in early in the morning. I thought you'd stay here in the shack for the night while I go home but there's no food here. I've got my Jeep there and we can run and get you something if you need it."

"I ate on the plane," Brian said. "And I have some stuff in the packs. I'll be fine."

"Good enough." He pulled the plane delicately to the dock, climbed out on the float and tied up the plane. "We'll be back early in the morning – I plan on leaving here at daylight-thirty. About four-thirty. See you." And he was gone.

Brian stood alone on the dock and looked at the shore. It was not woods. Not yet. Here and there were cabins, and docks with boats next to them. But there were thick trees and bird sounds and green – lord, he'd forgotten how thickly green the northern forest is in the summer – and he let the sounds, and the lack of noise, settle over him like a blanket. He stood there for perhaps five minutes, relaxing.

It was coming into evening. He purposely had not brought a watch or clock. They did not fit where he would be. And he had been only partially honest with the pilot. He *had* eaten on the plane – a tiny sandwich and some peanuts and a Coke – but he didn't have food with him. Instead he had the ability to get food.

He took his pack with the sleeping bag out of the plane and moved up to the small building. It was unlocked and inside it was full of old engine parts and fishing gear. There was a couch in one corner and he thought of sleeping on it. But the sky didn't look like rain and the stink from paint cans in the corner convinced him. He would sleep away from the shack.

In one pocket of the pack he had rolls of fishing line, small sinkers and a plastic container of hooks. He had seen many small panfish – bluegills and sunfish – by the dock when he stepped off the plane float and he rigged a line with a hook and sinker. Then he went into the trees, turned over a rotting log and grabbed half a dozen earthworms.

The fish seemed starved and in ten minutes he'd caught five of them. He pulled the line, rolled it on a stick and put it back in his pack. Then he cleaned the fish, leaving the heads on, scaled them with the back of his knife and threw them in his smaller pot. The shore was covered with driftwood and in moments he had a small cooking fire going near the water's edge on the small strip of sand beach. He added lake water to the pot, slapped the lid on and put it directly into the flames.

The evening crop of mosquitos found him but he threw some green grass and leaves on the fire. The smoke drove them away. He sat and watched the evening sun disappear over the lake to his left, and thought how truly and honestly right it felt.

Once, when he didn't think he could stand being at home any longer, in the middle of the night he had taken the blanket off his bed and gone into the backyard and lain on the ground. It was almost more than he could bear to be in a room without an open window. He had to feel the air on his skin, to feel a part of the outside. That night he had lain trying to see up to the sky, to the stars. There was too much city light to see much but he tried, just as he tried to pretend the air in the yard was the same as the air in the woods.

Now he spread his bag in the grass on the bank and lay on it. It was not dark yet but close, and he could make out an evening star and he thought of how people wished on them. He had never done it but now he wished he could see it again the next night and the next and the next and always be able to see it.

He smelled his fish soup. It was nearly done and he added a couple of pinches of salt from a plastic bag he had brought and set the pot off the fire to cool a little.

After ten minutes he took the lid off and used the tip of his knife and a spoon to peel the skin away, then ate the tender pink meat along the backbones.

He ate quickly, carefully avoiding the bones, and then drank the broth. He cleaned his pan in the lake and decided to put up his tent to avoid the night bugs. He'd brought a small two-man tent. He'd thought of going without one at first but the tent was very light and had screened openings and the insects – whether he loved the woods or not – were awful. It took him five minutes to set it up and put his bag inside but instead of going to bed at once he put more driftwood on the fire and sat for a while in the dark.

He was close now. Not quite there but very close. Tomorrow the plane would take him northeast. He smiled.

He unzipped the tent and crawled inside and lay on top of the bag. For the first time in months he was sound asleep within five minutes.

NINE

Brian awakened and for a second did not remember where he was. There was a scuffling outside and he thought of bear and how stupid he'd been to leave his pack on the ground next to the tent. When he looked out he saw not a bear but a skunk and it wasn't near his pack but smelling around the dead embers of the fire.

The fish leftovers. When he'd finished the soup he'd put the skins and heads and bones on the fire and burned them. The smell must have traveled up and down the lakeshore. There was half a moon and enough light to make out what was happening. He sat up to watch and the movement startled the skunk, which immediately raised its tail and aimed at him – from six feet away – but held fire.

Brian sat very still and the skunk seemed to shrug and then lowered its tail and went back to snooping around the fire. When it didn't find anything it looked once more at the screened tent, snorted and waddled off into the night.

Brian smiled as he watched it leave. He didn't

know if it was a female but thought of it that way because the only other skunk he'd known closely had been a female that had "adopted" him and moved in with him when he'd spent the winter in the North. She had saved him from a bear and he would always have a soft spot for skunks.

In the east the sky was faintly light and Brian decided to get up and get ready. The pilot had said daylight-thirty and that would be in not much over an hour.

He made a small fire and put some water on to boil and dropped a pinch of tea in the water. While it was heating and boiling he rolled his bag and took the tent down and repacked it.

For a time he had nothing to do and he sat watching the fire, feeling hunger come back. The fish and broth had filled him but hadn't lasted long and he didn't have time now to fish and cook before it was time to leave. Hunger was an old friend. Once it had been an enemy and he had panicked whenever he felt the edges of it, but now he knew he wouldn't die if he didn't eat right away, or even this day, and he mentally tightened his belt.

Besides, he had some sugar cubes. He put three of them in the tea and drank it out of the pot as soon as it had cooled enough, and the hunger was knocked down.

He used the empty pot to pour water on the fire,

killed it completely and stirred the ashes into slush. Then he loaded his pack and sleeping bag back on the plane and sat on the dock waiting.

Somewhere nearby a loon called for the morning, the sound flowing gently across the lake, and it seemed then, for a moment, as if he'd never been gone. As if the past two years and more had not existed and he'd stayed in the bush.

This lasted until he heard a motor and looked up to see an old Jeep Cherokee rattling down the ruts to the shack. There was a canoe on top and the pilot and two men inside.

Brian stood and waited as the Jeep parked. The three of them got out and took the canoe down and moved onto the dock.

He'd been dreading meeting the fishermen. All the magazines he'd read and some of the shows he'd watched on television had left a bad taste in his mouth about so-called professional fishermen. He didn't feel like explaining himself to anybody. The pilot knew who he was, knew the Smallhorns and that he was going to visit them – or assumed it. Now there were two others who would ask questions.

But Brian was wrong.

The men were old – past sixty – but still moving well. They took the canoe down and tied it on the off float of the plane, the one away from the dock, with practiced ease. They looked so much alike that Brian thought they must be brothers. Square-jawed and balding; what hair they had was gray and bristly. They smiled easily, said hello to Brian, but didn't ask more from him.

The plane was almost full by the time the men got their gear behind the rear seat. Brian moved his packs back as well and slid into the rear seat. The plane only took four adults so one of the old men sat next to him and oddly enough it was Brian who wanted to question them. Their fishing equipment wasn't new or high-tech. The reels were old casting reels, obviously well kept, and the men handled them with an almost loving care.

Brian was silent until they were in the air and then he turned to the man next to him. "Do you fish a lot?"

The man had been looking out the window, down at the lakes, and he turned and smiled. "Once a year. We go up into the bush lakes and fish for muskies. We catch and release them – actually, we hardly ever catch them because we cast and use plugs we made ourselves. I haven't caught one now in . . . Ben, when did I last catch a muskie? Was it two years ago?"

The man in the front turned. "Yes. No. I think it was three. We've had a lot of strikes since then but no boaters. Why?"

"I was just telling the boy about our fishing."

"Nonfishing, you mean. We never seem to catch anything."

The man next to Brian nodded. "But we see the country and that's what it's all about, isn't it?" He studied Brian, his eyes questioning.

"Yes." Brian looked out the window. "That's what it's all about . . ."

"We worked the woods all our lives." Ben, the man in front, turned. "Cruising for the lumber companies, living. Just living. We're down in the Cities now but once you've been in the woods – well, you can take the man out of the woods, but you can't take the woods out of the man. We like to get back. Muskie fishing is just an excuse."

The man next to Brian nodded. "It must be the same for you. We heard about you, saw it all on television back when it happened. You must have got the woods in you then."

Brian nodded.

"It's a wonderful thing," the old man said, looking again out the window.

"What?"

"To have the woods in you. Young people almost never have it now. You're very lucky."

And Brian knew he was right. He'd never felt he was particularly fortunate before but the old man was exactly right. He was very lucky to have the woods in him and to be getting back to it. "I hope you have good fishing," he said, and meant it.

"And you as well. I hope everything comes to you that you want."

Brian smiled and watched the woods and lakes unroll beneath the plane. The droning of the engine made him drowsy and his eyes closed, then opened again, and he thought – looking across the wilderness, half-asleep – he thought, lord, what a wonderful place this is, and knew it was a kind of prayer.

The List

CANOE, 17-foot, Kevlar, named The Raft, from my time with Derek on the river. With two wide wood paddles with glassed tips. Repair kit with a piece of glass cloth and epoxy resin. Light life-vest flotation device.

STRAIGHT BOW, Wood-and-glass-laminated, 45-pound pull at 26-inch draw, 4 extra strings. 100 cedar arrow shafts, all spine tested for stiffness to match the bow. 60 field points, 50 MA-3 broadheads, nocks, precut 4-inch feathers – turkey, not plastic – glue to make everything, point cement, small fletcher to put feathers on, plastic tapering tool to work shafts down to take the points and nocks.

He debated long on the arrows – whether to take premade arrows or the materials to make them and in the end did both. He had two dozen finished arrows, half broadheads and half field points.

Small stone and file to sharpen broadheads. Plain leather quiver to hang down the center of my back.

Again, he debated whether to use a standard over-the-shoulder quiver or a center-hung with double harness. He decided on the center quiver because his head would protect the arrows and keep them from hitting things when he was moving through the brush.

KNIFE, Plain hunting-style knife with cross hilt and straight 6-inch flat blade sharpened on one side except for the tip, to be sharpened also on the top back about 2 inches. A tool – and a weapon. Use the same stone and file for sharpening the broadheads to sharpen the knife and hatchet.

HATCHET

There were many variations he could have gone with here, as with knives, but he chose a plain belt ax, not unlike the one his mother had given him when he started north the first time. Like the knife,

53

it was always on his belt and would always be there. He had learned that it was much better to have a tool-weapon with you and not need it than it was to need one and not have it.

FISHING GEAR, Nothing fancy. 2 spools of braided line, 20-pound test, a dozen metal leaders and a container of small sinkers, the kind with the rubber twist center. Small plastic box with 100 assorted fishhooks. No rod, no reel, just the hooks, line and sinkers.

At this point in compiling the List a kind of stubbornness had come into Brian's thinking. He had lived before with much less – just having a modern bow and good arrows and real fishing gear was like being rich – and part of him wanted to just go with that. Maybe throw in a pot for cooking and of course some clothes. But he had not been completely idle in the two and a half years since he'd been "lost in the wilderness", as some put it. He had been reading, expanding his knowledge, and most of the reading he'd done had been not about modern survival gurus or people who used high-tech gear to go off for a week or a month and then write a book or do a documentary about it and get rich. He had instead studied the true winners, the people in history who had survived in the wild because they had no other choice – the primitive

Native Americans of the past, as well as Inuit, Cree and even the peoples of the U.S. Southwest, though the terrain in that region was radically different from these north woods. For them it wasn't a game but their lives; what Brian knew now as primitive living had in fact been modern for them. It was how they lived – or died. He read and reread and in the end decided that if those people had had modern conveniences available they would have used them – just as they did when new things came along. Very few Native Americans still chipped stone arrowheads to use for hunting, though he suspected some of them still hunted with a bow.

Brian decided he would still draw a line. If he went crazy and took everything available – guns, water makers, special clothing or gear – he would lose what he had found, the beauty, the connection with the wild that had come into him.

So he added carefully to the List:

BOOKS, Compact 2-volume set of the complete works of Shakespeare. Definitive guide, with pictures, of edible plants, nuts and berries of the north woods.

He had come to love reading as much as he disliked television and he'd chewed on which books to take – they were heavy and could not stand much rough use – and decided to ask Caleb, who in turn had asked him, "Who is the greatest writer of all?" Brian had been stumped until Caleb told him.

"Shakespeare."

"I've never been able to read him."

"Well then, now is a good time to start," Caleb said. "And when you do, read aloud."

"Even alone?"

"It's easier to understand. They're plays, meant to be read aloud. Just try it."

He had learned a lot on his own in his time in the woods – sometimes with disastrous results – and he brought the field guide because he wanted to have a wider knowledge of what he could safely eat. Shakespeare for the soul, the guide for the stomach.

3 mechanical pencils with extra lead. 4 small books with blank lined pages.

He didn't usually keep a journal, and he didn't want to lock himself into it now. But he had become very close to Caleb, in some ways closer than he was to his parents, and he thought he could keep a running letter to Caleb and instead of trying to send him pages in envelopes, he could send the book all at once when he found a way to get it out.

CAMPING GEAR AND SUPPLIES, 1 good compass.

He thought of taking a Global Positioning

System which relies on satellite signals, but had a distrust of complicated systems and decided against it. One drop of water in the wrong place or a fall or dropping it on the rocks and it was useless. Besides, he would have a good map from the pilot and every lake was a landmark.

2 decent-quality backpacks with external frames.
1 small camp shovel.

Here the concept of world politics helped him. The Soviet Union had come apart and one of the things its crumbling military complex had was surplus titanium. Some enterprising Russian had come up with the idea of making titanium – superlight and superstrong – camping shovels and Brian bought one through a catalog.

1 small but good-quality 2-man tent, the kind that becomes a dome with a screen entrance.

He was not sure how long it would last – probably until the first bear decided to tear it apart – but it would give him a chance to sleep mosquito-free for a while.

Sleeping bag rated to 0 degrees.

This was much too warm for a summer bag but in the back of his mind were the fall and winter nights, the still, deep cold. For now he could always open the bag and sleep on top of it.

2 aluminum pots, a 2-quart and a 4-quart, with lids. A large metal insulated cup. A 2-quart plastic water container.

No frying pan, no oil. No stove. He'd become accustomed to cooking over fire and preferred it. Besides, if he used a cooking stove he'd have to carry fuel for it and that was a whole new problem.

A container of salt in a plastic bag.

He had missed salt a great deal in the bush.

3 boxes sugar cubes in a plastic bag.

For his sweet tooth.

3 boxes of 1-gallon zip-closure plastic bags. Tea for several months. 4 plastic bottles vitamin C tablets and 3 bottles of multiple vitamins.

He hadn't had vitamins the first time out, but his mother and Caleb had insisted on it. His mother didn't know Brian would be on his own for a time, perhaps for a long time, but she wanted him to take the vitamins anyway. "Don't those people you're going to visit use vitamins?"

"Smallhorns. They are the Smallhorns, Mother, not 'those people'."

58

"Whatever. Surely they use vitamins. You take them."

A 25-pound bag brown rice, wrapped in a plastic garbage bag. A roll of 30 plastic garbage sacks to waterproof equipment and packs.

In his reading he'd discovered that most of the cultures in the world seemed to exist on rice and he had started to cook with it at home, though in small amounts. His mother didn't like it. He found it bland but mixable with other foods and he thought to use it now and then with fish or other meat or wild vegetables.

No flour, no bread, no candy, no ingredients for pizza – Caleb had jokingly suggested that one – no ice cream, no soda. None of the things he had come to miss so much when he was in the woods before. They had all proved to be phony pleasures. He neither wanted them nor needed them in his life any longer.

A small, basic first-aid kit.

He couldn't do sutures or treat major wounds with this but he had filled a prescription for antibiotics to help with any infection he might get. Also insect repellant.

8 boxes waterproof matches. 3 small propane lighters.

He remembered the difficulty of getting a fire going and while he felt certain he could do it again with just the hatchet and a stone, this was one area where he definitely wanted to go modern. He'd also brought a magnifying glass to look closely at things that might interest him and he could use it to start fires if the sun was out.

CLOTHING, 2 pairs loose hiking pants. A pair of soft hiking shoes. 4 T-shirts. 2 pullover Polar Fleece jackets. A pullover breathable, waterproof anorak with a hood. A fabric military-style belt to carry the knife and hatchet. 3 pairs athletic socks. 3 pairs hiking shorts with several pockets. 3 pairs briefs. 2 billed caps. A sewing kit with assorted needles and 4 spools heavy thread. 1 spool waxed sewing cord with heavy needles. A hand-awl needle combination. 3 small cakes beeswax for thread and bowstrings.

If it came to it he wanted to be able to sew leather, especially for moccasins. Hiking shoes were fine but he had come to like sewn moccasins – they were light and though they wore out rapidly he could feel the ground through them and move more quietly.

A 10-by-10-foot tarp. 200 feet of 1/8-inch nylon rope – parachute cord.

And an old 3-pound coffee can he found in the water by the plane when they were getting ready to take off from Ranier.

TEN

Dear Caleb: I had surprise company today. She didn't stay long, which I'm glad about, but she definitely kept me from being bored.

And now he was, at last, alone.

He held the canoe in the lily pads and let the smoke from the small fire in the can blow over him and take the mosquitos away. There were fish everywhere. Hiding beneath the pads he could see dozens of bluegills and other panfish – sunfish, he thought, from the yellow flash of their bellies when they turned suddenly – and now and then a northern pike hunting the lilies would hit them and scatter them. He would take some later for food but it was only midafternoon and the plane had just gone – he thought he could still hear the engine – and he had time to move to the end of this small lake before dark and time to camp.

He smiled remembering the pilot when they'd landed. He had dropped the other two men off first – a lighter plane used less fuel – so the two of them had been alone for the flight. It had taken forty minutes or so to fly a hundred miles and the noise of the engine was loud so they didn't speak much.

At one point the pilot leaned over and yelled, "You sure you'll be all right alone up here?"

As right as I've ever been, Brian thought, and was going to yell it but simply nodded and that was all their conversation until they landed and taxied to a stop at the end of the lake.

"You're here." The pilot took a map from a folder in the back and handed it to Brian. "This little lake is called Payson Lake. You need to work this stream north up to Liberty Lake and then this series of chain lakes" – he unfolded the map – "up to Williams Lake. The Smallhorns are in camp here. They were at the northeast end but it's a fish camp and they move around the lake. You can see it's a big lake – I think eight or nine miles long and a couple wide – so you might have to look for them."

He gave Brian the map and helped him unload his canoe and put his gear in it. Before doing anything else, still standing on the float of the plane, Brian folded the map so his locale was faceup and put it in one of the plastic bags to keep it waterproof. Then he waded ashore.

"See you in the fall," the pilot called.

He waited until Brian was well away from the

plane, then fired up the engine and took off without looking back.

Brian had moved at once to the shore of the small lake, pulled the canoe up on a grassy flat area and repacked his equipment. He tied everything that was loose in the canoe to the cross-strut and covered it all with the tarp except for his bow and the quiver of arrows. If he fell or the canoe rolled he would not lose all his gear. He strung the bow, made certain the string was properly nocked at both ends, and put it within easy reach on the tarp. It wasn't tied down but the bow and arrows floated and wouldn't be lost if the canoe rolled over suddenly.

It was hot and Brian stripped to a pair of shorts, taking his T-shirt off and rolling it under the tarp. The life jacket was nearby but since he would be working near the shore in three feet of water and then up a small creek he didn't feel like wearing it. It was not the safest thing to do – and he would wear it if he started into deep water – but the sun felt so nice on his bare skin that he wanted to be free for a time. For the same reason he took off his cap and rolled it up in a side pocket on one of the packs. The flies and mosquitos were bad – as bad as he'd ever seen them – but the little whiff of smoke now and then from the can in the bottom of the canoe kept them at bay.

He did not hurry. He thought he might never hurry again and he quickly dropped into what he sometimes thought of as woods time. It wasn't about time so much as about knowing what was happening and where it was happening. He often remembered the wolf he had seen moving through the woods, listening to everything, seeing everything, taking its time to not miss whatever there was to see.

Brian did that now. A leaf that moved, a small bit of wind, the cry of a small bird – he breathed slowly, quietly, and paddled the canoe gently along the shore. He saw and heard it all, was as absolutely tuned to the woods as he'd ever been, and so was completely surprised when the deer jumped into the canoe.

ELEVEN

Dear Caleb: Today I found out about plans and how they don't always work.

There was a sudden crash to his side – so fast he hadn't heard any preliminary movement – and a whitetail doe flew out of the brush to his right. She was a full eight feet in the air when she left the brush and billowing from her eyes were clouds of something that resembled smoke. Later, when he had time to think, he decided that flies and mosquitos were attacking her eyes, and she was momentarily blinded.

She was trying to make the water, where she could put her head under and clear away the bugs.

She landed almost exactly in the center of the canoe, nearly in Brian's lap. And she wanted out.

Brian had read about a man who had accidentally hit a buck with his station wagon. The deer was knocked sideways and lay still in the ditch. The man stopped. Thinking the deer was dead, and not wanting to waste the meat, he put the deer in the back of the station wagon. He'd gone about four miles when the deer, which was only stunned, came back to life. The man said it was like a bomb had gone off in the car. To save himself he opened the door and bailed out with the car still moving. The deer kicked out every window, including the windshield, before it could get out and get away.

Something close to that happened now to Brian. The doe landed half on her feet and half on her stomach across the canoe. Her head, which was over the side, went down in the water and she thrashed around to raise it – probably thinking she was on a log of some kind – to find herself staring directly into Brian's eyes.

It was impossible to say who was more surprised.

"Hey—" Brian just had time to start when with a lunge and a kick the doe left the canoe. The problem was that her back feet caught the gunwale of the canoe and spun it like a cork.

In half a second Brian went from being upright with not a care in the world, thinking how wonderful and grand everything was, to being upside down, lungs full of water, tangled up in canoe, gear, lily pads and mud.

"Arrrgghh!" He came up screaming and spitting mud and water. "What . . ."

He still hadn't figured out quite what had happened but it rapidly became clear as he saw the deer bounding up out of the water and away into the brush on the shore while he stood, waist deep, surrounded by arrows, bow, upside-down canoe and packs – still dry inside garbage bags.

Nothing was seriously damaged.

Nearby onshore was a small clearing ten or twelve yards across. Brian grabbed the side of the canoe and dragged it up to the shore. He untied the packs and put them on the grass, along with his bow and arrows and the extra paddle. The equipment in the packs had been enclosed in plastic but he had neglected to wrap his sleeping bag so it was wet, though not soaked through. It had been in its stow bag and water seeped in only at the end – still, it needed to be dried.

"Well, I guess," he said, looking around at the clearing, "that's one way to find a camping spot."

He flipped the canoe and emptied it, pulled it up on the grass and inverted it again. He spread his sleeping bag in the sun to dry and put his tent up.

There were fish in the lily pads and Brian put the line out with a bare hook, standing in the water up to his waist and fishing out around his legs. The hook was golden and flashed tiny bits of light. The fish bit without bait and he took half a dozen hand-size panfish. They were a mix of bluegills and a smaller brownish fish that seemed to be a cousin of a crappie – maybe some kind of rock bass – but they would taste fine. He cleaned and scaled them and put them in the large pan with fresh water.

He gathered dry driftwood for half an hour and had plenty for the night. He started a fire and put the fish on one side of the fire and then he put one cup of water in the small pot with half a cup of rice and put it on the other side of the flames. He had not eaten since the night before and would get a full meal for tonight.

The fish boiled fast and was done in fifteen minutes. The rice took about half an hour. Brian picked the meat off the fish and put it in his metal cup until the rice was done; then he added the fish and some salt to the rice. He ate with a spoon, cleaned the pot well, then boiled water in the large pot to fill his two-quart canteen for the next day and furnish him with a cup of evening tea.

While the water was boiling he bearproofed the camp, or did the best he could. He had read up on bears when he was back in civilization and knew that above all they were intelligent and unpredictable. To be secure you had to get rid of all food smells. He buried the fish bones and skin well away from the camp area. He then tied the end of a piece of nylon rope to a stick to give it weight and lobbed it over a limb thirty feet up in a nearby birch. He tied both his packs to the line and pulled them up fifteen feet in the air, then snubbed the line off. A smart bear might know to chew the rope off and drop the packs, but he doubted there were many that intelligent around.

His sleeping bag was dry and he put it in the tent, then sat by the fire sipping hot tea with a sugar cube while he checked his bow. The string was well waxed and the water had not penetrated it. The bow itself was finished with a varnish that was waterproof. The arrows were a different story. They were made of bare wood – he hadn't bothered to paint them or varnish the shafts – and the feathers had become soaked. He checked each shaft carefully to make certain it was still straight, found two that were slightly off and bent them gently until they were straight while holding them to the heat. All this knowledge came from books he'd read on old-time archery.

He then carefully held each arrow so that heat from the fire dried the feathers without curling them. It was a painstaking process, and he took his time, listening to the crackle of the fire, adding a stick or two now and then and becoming more and more aware of the night woods around him.

The forest was alive, for the woods became more active in the dark. Many predators were nocturnal – it was easier to catch prey then – though many prey animals like mice and rabbits moved in the dark because they felt safer.

Brian heard a hundred rustlings, rubbings, breaking of small twigs, brushing of hair against leaves. There, he thought, was a squirrel moving through trees, and there was a mouse or a rabbit moving over the forest floor – it was hard to tell them apart.

Suddenly he heard a scream, far off, as a rabbit was caught and died. It sounded almost human, babylike, very much like the sound a baby doll makes when it is tipped over. He heard it twice and then the rabbit was gone, into a wolf or fox or skunk or weasel, perhaps even an owl. Rabbits and mice were the bottom of the food chain in the woods – everybody ate them – and he heard screams twice more.

Three dead rabbits. As he held an arrow to the heat he let his mind play with the numbers. Three dead rabbits in an hour. He could probably only hear them scream from a couple of hundred yards – say a quarter of a square mile around him. Which meant that perhaps six rabbits an hour were killed in every square mile of wilderness at night and yet there were still hundreds, thousands of rabbits running loose, so many that in winter they left small highways packed so hard they would hold a human up on the snow.

He shook his head. Wasted thought. There were rabbits. They were good to eat. He had eaten many of them. He would eat many more. It was enough.

It was late and the moon was up. When he finished drying the arrows and quiver, he put the fire out and took his weapons and bow into the tent.

He was suffering a kind of jet lag, the shock of coming from civilization to the bush, and he was very tired. He crawled into his bag, arranged the knife and hatchet and bow and arrows near his head and leaned back and down to sleep.

It was a few minutes coming. He lay listening to the woods, thinking of the day. He hadn't planned to camp here. On the map it was only a few miles to the next lake and he'd thought to go there before camping but the doe had come along and changed all his plans.

She had picked the campsite for him, he thought, smiling, as sleep came over him and he closed his eyes and let the day slip away.

TWELVE

Dear Caleb: Today I saw a place that was so beautiful that I don't think even Shakespeare could describe it.

The map showed a series of small lakes covering perhaps thirty miles. In between, from lake to lake, there appeared to be a meandering river, all of it equally divided so that a lake might be three or four miles long, then the river to the next lake another three or four miles. But Brian was to find that the map wasn't accurate.

He awakened just after dawn, when the sun began to warm the tent. The sky was cloudless. He flipped the canoe and when he went to lower his packs he saw the bear tracks.

One bear, medium size. It had come in the night so quietly that Brian hadn't heard it – though he had slept so soundly the bear could have been tipping garbage cans.

It had done no damage. The tracks went by the fire, then moved to where he'd buried the fish leftovers. The bear had dug them up and eaten them. It had moved to the tent, apparently looked in on him, then gone to the packs. Brian could see that it had tried to stand and reach them. There were claw marks on the tree but the bear had never figured out the rope holding the packs and had gone off without doing anything destructive.

"Company," he said. "And I didn't even wake up."

He slid the canoe into the water at the edge of the lake and loaded all his gear, again tying everything in. He took time to gather some bits of wood and leaves for a smudge in the can, then jumped in. It was still early but already warm and he quickly stripped down to shorts.

He kept the map in its clear plastic bag jammed beneath a rope in front of him. He knelt to paddle instead of sitting on the small seat because it felt more stable. He was not as confident in the canoe as he wished to be. He'd taken it to a small lake near home to practice and rented canoes in other places, but the ease with which the doe had flipped him made him very conscious of the fact that he had much to learn. By staying low and on his knees he had much more control.

He sat toward the rear with the load tied in slightly forward of the middle, which kept the canoe nearly level and easy to steer and control. He studied the map as he paddled.

He had only a mile to go in the present lake and then he would enter the river. He had the compass in one of the packs but didn't truly need it. The lakes were well drawn on the map and he could see where the river flowed out.

Except that it wasn't a river.

Brian worked easily to the end of the lake but when he came to the point where the river was supposed to flow out he found that there was no current. Instead of a series of different lakes connected by small rivers, the land was level and flat. It was all just one long lake and the very narrow portions that showed on the map as rivers really were long, tranquil ponds.

They were so narrow that the trees had grown together over them and Brian found himself paddling through a green wonderland.

The water was absolutely still beneath the trees. He could see his reflection ahead of him and off to the side, so distinct it was as if he were gliding over a mirror. And the water was clear. On both edges were lily pad forests and beneath them he could see where schools of panfish lay hidden. Inside of half an hour he saw a muskie that had to be thirty or forty pounds hunting the edges of the pads.

Overhead the trees were filled with birds and they sang all at the same time. The sound blended into a kind of music and Brian found himself humming with it as he paddled.

Halfway through the first of the long, covered passageways he came upon a cow moose. She was well off to the side and had her head completely under water pulling at lily pad roots. As Brian came upon her, gliding silently, she raised her head suddenly and seemed to stare directly at him.

Brian had run into difficulties in the past with moose. He thought they were insane, and he'd been attacked by them twice. He laid the paddle down softly and took up his bow. He had kept one of the broadheads lying across the pack by the bow. Moving slowly, he fitted the arrow to the string so if need be he could grab the bow and get at least one arrow into the moose if she charged.

He passed not twenty feet from her but all she did was keep chewing on the root, water dripping in golden drops from her muzzle, breaking the surface like jewels. It was as though she hadn't seen him – and perhaps she hadn't. Moose, he had read, had terrible eyesight and she may have thought he was merely a log drifting by. Before he had passed by, she had put her head beneath the surface again, looking for more roots. Brian went back to studying beauty.

All that day he felt as if he were in a painting, a beautiful private diorama. He worked through a sheltered narrow lagoon and then out into the open to cross a small lake, then back under the canopy through the still water.

He had never had a day pass so quickly nor so beautifully and he nearly forgot that he had to find a camp and get some food before dark. He wasn't sick of boiled fish and rice yet, so in the late afternoon he took time to move back along the lily pads and drop the hook over. He caught a large sunfish immediately – again, on a bare hook – and took three more small ones, dropping them all over the side using a short piece of nylon rope as a stringer, running the nylon through their gills and out their mouths.

He took his time looking for a campsite and picked one on a flat area five or six feet above the surface of the lake. It was a clearing about twenty yards across. There were many such clearings, probably all made by beaver cutting down the small trees years before, allowing the grass to take over. Brian pulled the canoe well up onto the grass and for no real reason tied a piece of line from the boat's bow to a tree.

Later he would wonder at this bit of foresight. He had not done it the night before, and since this site was much higher from the water he wouldn't have thought he'd need to secure the canoe here.

The storm hit in the middle of the night.

THIRTEEN

*Dear Caleb: Nothing much to report today,
unless you count shooting yourself in the leg
with an arrow . . .*

It was not that there was so much wind – certainly not as much as he'd been through before with the tornado – when he was first marooned in the wilderness and not that there was so much rain, although there was a goodly amount of it.

It was the combination of the two.

He had cooked dinner and eaten, boiled water for the next day's canteen, pulled his packs up in a tree, set up the tent and arranged his sleeping bag and weapons. Then he'd sat by the fire and written to Caleb about the day in one of the books, using tiny writing so he wouldn't waste the pages.

When he was done he put the book back in a plastic bag and crawled inside the tent to go to bed.

Two things he noted but didn't pay attention to: One, the mosquitos and flies were not as bad as they'd been. Two, with darkness a heavy cloud layer had come up, causing a closeness in the air.

He had studied the map. It looked as if he'd gone more than twenty miles, which explained why he was tired. About eighty miles remained to reach Williams Lake, maybe four more days at his current rate. He fell asleep almost as soon as he lay down.

He was awakened by a new sound, a loud sound. Not thunder – it never did thunder or lighten – and not the trainlike roar of a tornado. This just started low, the hissing of rain driven against the tent. He listened for a moment, then snuggled back in his bag. He was in a good shelter, waterproof – let it rain.

Except that it kept coming and *kept* coming. It went from a moderate rain to a downpour and finally to an outright deluge. And with the rain came wind. Not violent, but enough to break off branches and push the rain still harder, and soon Brian found his bag wet as the rain came in under the tent. He lifted the flap to look out but it was far too dark to see anything.

And it rained harder. And harder. The wind pushed stronger and still stronger and at last the tent seemed to sigh. It collapsed around him and he started rolling across the grass toward the edge of the clearing.

Everything was upside down, crazy. He couldn't find the entrance and about the time he thought he

had it the tent dropped off the five-foot embankment and he rolled down to the lakeshore.

He landed in a heap and felt an intense, hot pain
in his right leg at the upper thigh and reached down
to feel an arrow shaft protruding from his leg.

Great, he thought. I've shot myself in the leg. He
hadn't, of course, but had rolled onto an arrow that
had fallen out of the quiver just as the tent rolled off
the embankment.

He couldn't get his bearings but he knew where
his thigh was and he grabbed the arrow and jerked
the shaft out of his leg. There was an immediate
surge of pain and he felt like passing out. He didn't,
but then he heard a strange *whump-thump* and
something crashed down on his head. This time he
did pass out.

He came to a few seconds later with a sore head,
a sore leg and absolutely no idea in the world what
was happening to him. He was still wrapped in the
tent and his bag was in his face and his bow and
arrows lay all around him and he seemed to be in
water, almost swimming.

All right, he thought, take one thing at a time.
Just one thing.

I poked my leg with an arrow.

There. Good. I pulled the arrow out. My leg still
works. It must not have been a broadhead because
it didn't go in very deep. Good.

My tent collapsed. There. Another thing. I'm in the tent and it collapsed. I just have to find the front zipper and get out and climb up the bank. Easy now, easy.

Something hit me on the head. What? Something big that thunked. The canoe. The wind picked up the canoe and it hit me.

There. I've poked my leg, rolled down a bank and been hit in the head with the canoe.

All simple things. All fixable things.

He fumbled around and at last found the zipper at the front of the tent, opened it and slithered out into the mud on the lakeshore.

The rain was still coming down in sheets, the wind still hissing and slashing him with the water, but he had his bearings and it was not impossible to deal with things. He dragged the tent back up the embankment onto the grass, limping as the pain in his leg hit him. It was too dark to see much but he could make out the shape of the canoe lying upside down. It had moved a good ten feet from where he had left it and had he not tied it down loosely with the line it would have blown away across the lake.

He had forgotten the most important thing about living in the wilderness, the one thing he'd thought he would never forget – expect the unexpected. What you didn't think would get you, would get you. Plan on the worst and be happy when it didn't come.

But he had done one thing right: He had tied the canoe to a tree. He dragged the tent to the canoe, crawled underneath and lay on the tent the rest of the night, listening to the wind and rain, wincing now and then with the pain in his leg and feeling stupid.

It was a long night.

FOURTEEN

Dear Caleb: I read some Shakespeare today. I think it changed my life . . .

It was a repair day, both for equipment and for himself.

Dawn was wet and dreary and it took him a full hour to find some dry wood and leaves and get a decent fire going – all the time castigating himself. Had he forgotten *everything*? He hadn't made a secure camp, hadn't dug a rain gutter around the tent, hadn't brought in wood so he'd have dry fire starter in the morning.

He limped through the woods around the campsite until he found a dead birch log with the bark still intact. Birchbark was nearly waterproof – it was what Native Americans used for canoes – and beneath the bark he broke off slivers of dry wood. He took a double armful of bark and slivers back to the campsite and after three attempts – he should have needed only one match, he told himself – he at last got a sputtering flame going.

Once the bark caught it went like paper dipped in kerosene and the wood caught and when the flames were going well he put on smaller pieces of the wet firewood. The flames dried the wood and started it burning and in another half hour he had a good blaze going.

He took a moment then to examine his leg. There was a clean puncture wound not more than half an inch deep and he took some disinfectant from the first-aid kit and dabbed it on the hole, put a Band-Aid on it and then went back to work.

The wind had dropped and the rain had eased to a few sprinkles now and then. He saw clear holes in the clouds. He spread the gear to dry, tying it to limbs with nylon cord. His sleeping bag was soaked through and the tent was a sloppy mess. He had to stay put so he set the tent back up, this time pegging it down and using the small shovel to dig a drainage ditch around the sides with a runoff ditch leading down to the lake.

The wind had tangled the packs in the tree limbs but they were still intact, and after some effort Brian untangled them and lowered them to the ground.

Again he dried arrows and the quiver and checked his bow. Then he launched the canoe and took about fifteen minutes to catch six good-size bluegills. He cleaned the fish, put them on to boil with a teaspoon or so of salt, put rice in the other pan and then suddenly found that all the work was done.

The sun was out – he could actually see steam coming up from his sleeping bag as it dried – and he lay back on the ground by the fire and went over what had happened. His leg throbbed in time with his thoughts as he learned yet again: Never assume anything, expect the unexpected, be ready for everything all the time.

And finally, no matter what he *thought* would happen, nature would do what it wanted to do. He had to be part of it, part of what it was really like, not what he or some other person thought it should be like.

He gathered wood for the night and spread it in the sun to dry, took the meat off the fish and mixed it with the rice and set it aside to cool – he sometimes liked to eat the rice cold – and lay in the sun nude (his shorts drying on a limb) and let the smoke from the fire keep the mosquitos off while he dozed, catching up on sleep he'd lost in the rain the night before.

He slept solidly for more than four hours. The fire was nearly out when he awakened and he put more wood on the coals and got them going again.

It was midafternoon and he ate the rice and fish, then made tea and had a cup with a sugar cube for dessert.

By evening his bag was dry. He put it in the tent, put on a T-shirt because he was feeling a bit sunburned, and his hand bumped one of the Shakespeare volumes.

"So I'll try reading it . . ."

He had been exposed to Shakespeare in school, briefly, and had not paid much attention. The play they had read was *Romeo and Juliet* and he knew it was about young people so he tried it again now.

He stood on the shore and read aloud, and felt silly at first. But because he liked Caleb and trusted him he kept going, staggering on until he came to the verse in act 2 where Juliet says:

> *O Romeo, Romeo, wherefore art thou Romeo?*
> *Deny thy father and refuse thy name,*
> *Or, if thou wilt not, be but sworn my love,*
> *And I'll no longer be a Capulet.*

Here a strange thing happened to Brian. Whenever he'd heard this part before – on television, in school – he'd thought she was looking for Romeo, wondering where he was, calling for him. But something brought the words, the meaning, to him as he stood there in the afternoon sun, reading it aloud out onto the lake, and he knew that was wrong, knew that she was instead calling on Romeo, asking him why he was a member of the wrong family, the Montagues, and if only he weren't . . .

And a few lines later he read Juliet saying:

What's in a name? That which we call a rose
By any other word would smell as sweet.

And Brian knew. It was as if his whole world had suddenly opened. He *knew* what Shakespeare was trying to tell him. Of Juliet's love for Romeo, of her torment and despair over the agony of the fight between the two families.

This man had written of these things hundreds of years before Brian was born, in a world so different from Brian's it might be on another planet, and Brian *knew* . . .

It shook him, standing there on the side of a lake in the northern wilderness reading a love story written more than three hundred years earlier, to *know* how they felt, how they hurt.

He closed the book and sat down on the grass, his legs crossed, the sun heading into evening, and thought of all the time he had wasted not knowing Shakespeare, and a tear slid down his cheek, a tear for Juliet and Romeo, a tear for Shakespeare, who he wished were still alive, a tear for his own loss and a tear for the beauty of knowing sadness . . .

FIFTEEN

Dear Caleb: It gets more and more beautiful. I think most of the city is leaving me . . .

He was not sure what, if anything, awakened him. Probably the fact that he had slept so hard during the day. Whatever the reason, in the dead middle of the night his eyes suddenly snapped open and he sat up, listening with his mouth open, breathing in shallow pulls to not make noise.

Nothing.

He leaned forward and unzipped the tent and looked out. Still nothing, at least nothing to hear. But the sight that met his eyes made him hold his breath.

The sky was clear, filled with stars, and the moon was half full and laid a silver streak across the lake – a white road that came across the water and called to him with such intensity that he closed the tent and moved to the canoe, turned it over and slid it out onto the water.

The night was cool enough that the mosquitos

stayed down. He stroked once with the paddle and the canoe slid out and away from the bank into the silver reflection of the moon out on the water.

Another pull, another slide across the still water, moving through liquid silver. A loon called. It seemed to come from somewhere to the left but the sound moved around until it filled the lake, mixed somehow with the moonlight and became almost visible. It hung there, the sound he could see in the moonlight, for half a minute; then the loon called again, or another answered it, and suddenly – close, on the far edge of the lake, only a hundred yards away – a wolf howled.

Long, sweet, and sad and happy and frightening and joyful all at once, a keening howl that started high and dropped low and ended almost hoarse.

The hair went up on the back of Brian's neck and he took a deep breath and answered the howl, trying to match the tones of it, starting high the same way and bringing it down as low as he could until it trailed off.

Then he waited. Ten seconds, twenty, a full minute and the wolf called again. Different this time. Low all the time, almost a moan.

And Brian answered.

Three more times they went back and forth and finally Brian waited until the wolf started its call and Brian matched it, harmonized with it, and they sang together that way, four more songs, a duet, boy and wolf in the moonlight, singing to beauty until at last the wolf grew tired of it and quieted. Brian called twice more but when he didn't get an answer he stopped.

The moon was dropping below the horizon at any rate and he paddled back to the campsite, pulled the canoe up, tied it off and went back in to bed.

He did not sleep at first but lay thinking of the wolf and the moonlight and the loon and when he closed his eyes and sleep started to come he thought he could see the wolf, or perhaps see as the wolf moving through the night, part of the night, the smells and sounds of the woods moving through the wolf like vapor, stopping to listen, moving on in a silent slide through the moonlight and forest, Brian and the wolf mixed, Brian-wolf, wolf-Brian.

Then sleep.

He awakened completely refreshed, having slept again past dawn. It was a clear morning and the side of the tent was warm from the sun and he rolled out and stretched and walked to the canoe to flip it over and slide it into the water when he saw the prints.

Two wolves had come into camp. One good-size, the other slightly smaller, and from the look of the tracks around the tent in the drainage ditch, around the canoe in the soft earth and beneath the packs they had investigated everything. They had also peed on the canoe and the tent – not a great deal, but enough so he'd know they had, a calling card – and then moved on.

Brian smiled. Either they were greeting him or, more likely, telling him he was a lousy singer. He finished packing the canoe and just before leaving went up and covered the two places where they'd left sign with his own. Hello to you too, he peed. Then he got into the canoe and slid off.

He had not gone a mile when he was back beneath the canopy, in the green world, and wondered how far it was to the next lake. On the map that lake was long – almost eight miles before he would come to his first portage, about a half mile to the next lake, which was at least six miles long. He thought perhaps he would do the two of them today, which would bring the distance to Williams Lake down to about sixty-five miles.

The canopy only lasted three or four miles and he came out onto the eight-mile lake. There was a slight breeze coming up, directly into his face, so he put on the life jacket and set to the paddle, heading right up the middle of the lake.

The work felt good, solid somehow. The pain in his leg was nearly gone and he was just noodling along, paddling the canoe across small lakes and down the green corridors, not really working, and it felt good to stretch his arms and bite deep with the paddle and take the wind.

He kept up a steady effort and seemed to be moving well – an illusion caused by the visual effect of the wind blowing small waves in the opposite direction that he was going – but it took him four hours to make the eight miles.

"I guess the wind must be stronger than it looks," he said, gliding into the calm area at the end of the lake where the portage started. "Half a day gone . . ."

He pulled the canoe up on the bank and considered the situation. He had to carry everything half a mile and he couldn't do it all at once.

He tied the tent inside the canoe near the center, and under the cross-thwarts he tied the paddles, centering their weight, and the bow and the quiver of arrows. There was a yoke for portaging built into the canoe, shaped to fit around the neck and rest on the shoulders.

He put one backpack up in a tree on a bear-proof rope, and the other one he slipped onto his back.

Then he moved to the canoe, flipped it belly-up and moved beneath it and took the weight of the yoke on his shoulders.

At first it felt as if his legs would sink into the ground.

But the canoe balanced well and when he started off he gained a momentum that kept him going. It only took him twenty minutes to walk the portage. There wasn't a trail – the grass had grown up and covered any tracks – but there was a long clearing and in the dim past somebody had taken an ax and cut marks in the trees to show the direction.

Probably, Brian thought, Native Americans when they trapped through here. The ax marks were very old, healed over and often nearly covered with bark, so some were just a dimple.

Still, it meant people had been here before and it made Brian wonder about them. Fifty years ago, he thought, or maybe more – seventy-five. The trees were huge pines, the marks well off the ground. Whoever had made them was probably gone now, dead, nothing left but his mark.

He left the canoe at the next lake, tied the pack up in a tree – though he hadn't seen any signs of bear – and, carrying the bow with an arrow ready and the quiver on his back, he went back for the other pack.

It took him only ten minutes to get back. He let the pack down, took the quiver off his back and put the pack back on, and with the quiver in one hand

and the bow with a broadhead nocked to the string in the other he started for the canoe.

He hadn't taken three steps when he saw the deer. It was a buck, horns in velvet, and it stopped, a young animal with a small rack.

Good meat, Brian thought – really good meat. The thought came automatically and he lowered the quiver to the ground softly, raised the bow and paused. The deer wasn't thirty feet away and seemed entirely unafraid, standing there. While Brian watched, it actually turned its head away and looked to where a bird had chattered on a limb.

It would have been an easy shot. A clean shot. You're mine, Brian thought, and his throat seemed to choke with it, the excitement. Mine. The arrow was in the bow, he raised the bow, drew the arrow, sighted it so he was looking over the broadhead straight at the deer's heart, and then he paused again. He eased the string up and lowered the bow.

Maybe in the fall. He could not keep the meat in the hot weather. He would get three or four meals and the rest would spoil. The skin wouldn't make leather and most of the meat would be wasted.

He had fish, all the fish he wanted, all he would need. He could take a rabbit or a grouse for different meat, but not the deer, not now. It would be a waste.

"Thank you," he said aloud, to the deer, to whatever hunting spirit was watching over him, had given him this chance at meat. "Thank you . . ."

The sound of his voice startled the buck but still it stood for another beat, two, three, then it turned and trotted off down the portage trail for thirty or forty yards before springing lightly off to the side.

"Thank you," Brian whispered, watching it leave.

SIXTEEN

Dear Caleb: I met a man today and he helped me find my medicine.

The deer was on his mind when he came to where he'd left the canoe. He looked out at the lake ahead of him. The wind had picked up a bit, still on his nose, and he would be lucky to make the other end by dark.

For a moment, standing there looking at the water, he actually thought, I'm behind schedule, and then remembered he had no schedule. He was there to learn, to seek, to find, to know. It could happen here or over there or by going backward. There was no time requirement.

He thought of the deer again and the thought made him think of meat other than fish. He was suddenly hungry and he decided to make camp at the portage and hunt for a grouse or a rabbit to make a rice stew – something heavier than fish.

He tied the canoe off to a tree high above the lake, pulled his packs up in the air, found firewood enough for the night, and though it was no longer cloudy he stacked a pile of wood beneath the canoe to stay dry so he could start a fire if it did rain.

Then he hunted.

He put the quiver on his back again, took the broadhead off the bow and put it back in the quiver, and because he was taking small game he pulled out a field point – they were sharp but had curved shoulders to cause shock and a faster death than the cutting edge of a broadhead – and laid the arrow on the bow.

He slipped into the woods. He was wearing tennis shoes and wished he had moccasins but they would have to serve. The green grass kept his feet quiet enough.

One step, another, slowly into the thick green. A yard, another yard, ten yards – he didn't have to worry about getting lost because he kept the lake on his left, visible now and then through the leaves.

He saw a rabbit almost at once, and could have hit it easily enough, but that would have ended the hunt and he was moving now, into the woods, slowly, like a knife being pulled through water, the forest closing back in on him, his eyes seeing every movement, his ears hearing every rustle.

This, he thought, is what I have become. A hunter. The need to hurry disappeared, the need to kill was not as important as the need to see all there was to see, and he worked the afternoon away until evening, perhaps two hours before dark. He had seen seven or eight rabbits, any one of which he could have had, and heard several grouse and seen four more deer, two of which he could have hit easily, but he had waited and now, as he turned back, a grouse jumped up in front of him, its wings thundering, and flew to a limb on a birch about twenty-five feet away.

Now it was time. He raised the bow, drew the arrow back, looked down the wooden shaft and saw, felt, where the arrow would hit, and released, all in one clean, fluid motion.

The arrow went where he was looking, took the grouse almost in the exact center of the body, drove it back off the limb, and it fell, flopping for a moment, in the grass beneath the tree.

"Thank you," Brian whispered as it died. "For the food, thank you."

He picked the bird up, pulled the arrow out and wiped it on the grass, then tied the grouse to his belt with a short piece of nylon cord and started back. He was done hunting now but kept the bow ready, the arrow on the string.

It was nearing dusk. The sun was well below the line of trees, though it was still light, and he had much to do – set up the tent, make a fire, cook dinner and write in the journal – and he picked up the pace and was near where he'd left the canoe, still in thick trees, when he smelled the smoke.

He stopped. It was pine smoke. He couldn't see it, or hear anything, but there was a definite odor of smoke. It went away, then returned when he moved.

How could there be fire? There was no storm, no lightning – which Brian had read caused most forest fires – and besides, with the recent rain it wasn't likely there would be a forest fire.

Still, it was there. Again. He moved forward a few steps, stopped, and started to step again when he heard a clink of metal on stone.

Somebody was there. Ahead. At the camp.

Brian crouched and moved again, one step at a time, carefully, quietly, until he was at the edge of the forest. He moved a limb aside and peered out.

A man sat crouching with his back to Brian. There was another canoe pulled up by Brian's, an old fiberglass standard twelve-footer with many hard miles on it, judging by its look. The man had pulled up more wood and had a fire going and a pot of water boiling. Brian could see the steam. There was no weapon showing, no other gear. Just the canoe, tipped upside down, and the man and the fire. The man had long gray hair streaked with black, no hat but a headband, and had his hair tied into a ponytail.

All that, Brian saw without moving, without speaking.

"You might as well come in by the fire," the man said without looking. "I ain't that much to look at and I've got potatoes boiling with an onion. We can add that grouse you've got and have some stew."

Brian jumped. The voice was old, gravelly, but it carried so that it seemed to come from everywhere. He realized he still had the bow raised, not aimed exactly, but ready, and he lowered it and stepped out of the thick brush and walked to the fire and laid his bow and still-nocked arrow down by his canoe. He had a million questions – who was this man? where did he come from? why was he here? – but he kept his mouth still and the answers came. The man came from the woods, he came in a canoe while Brian was hunting, he was there as Brian was there – because he was there – and his name didn't matter, just as Brian's name didn't matter, and so he didn't ask.

But one thing puzzled Brian and this he did ask. "How did you know I had a grouse?"

"Smelled it. Your arrow hit the stomach and carried some of it through. Nothing smells like grouse guts."

"Ahh . . ." The wind was blowing right to carry the smell around the lake back to the campsite. Still, the man must have a very sensitive nose.

Brian moved down to the edge of the lake and cleaned the grouse. He tore the skin off with the feathers and washed the carcass in the water. He looked back up the bank out of the corner of his eye as he worked, studying his visitor. He was an older man – Brian guessed at least fifty – with a lined face darkened by smoke and weather. Perhaps he was from a native people. His face showed that he'd been in the woods a very long time. He had on worn moccasins, faded work pants and a work shirt buttoned up to the collar and buttoned at the cuffs. Everything, like his canoe, was old but in good repair. The shirt had been patched several times, the patches sewn neatly by hand with small stitches. His hands looked as if they were made of old polished wood.

"They call me Billy," the man said, still looking down at the fire.

"I'm Brian." He brought the grouse back to the fire and used his knife to cut it into pieces and dropped them into the stew pot, an old aluminum pot that could hold at least three gallons. The potatoes were just starting to boil.

Brian lowered his packs and sleeping bag. He found a little salt and started to put it in the stew and stopped. "Salt all right?"

"Some."

He put a bit in – less than he would have liked –

101

then took one of his own pots, the large one, and put tea and drinking water on to boil.

They did not talk. When the stew was done they each fished some out into their cups – Billy had his own tin cup, old and not insulated, though the heat didn't seem to bother his mouth – and they ate until it was all gone, including the broth. Brian buried the grouse bones off in the woods and they sat back and drank tea and watched the fire.

It was dark now, the moon not up yet, and they were silent for a long time. Brian was lost in thought, surprised to find he was thinking idly of his mother and Caleb. Here he was, sitting by a fire with this strange man, and it seemed the most natural thing in the world to be thinking about his mother. He wondered what she was doing.

"You hunt the old way," Billy said. It wasn't a question but a statement.

"Pardon?"

"With a bow. You hunt the old way. You don't use a gun."

Brian shook his head. "I don't like them. They make too much shock, no, too much . . . noise."

"They're wrong for the animal." Billy talked with his hands as well as his voice, the palms waving and the fingers pointing, dancing with the words as he spoke in almost music. "Too fast. Damn guns kill too quick, don't give them time to think about their place, time to face east. They don't get into the next world right when they get blown up. Arrows kill slower, give them time to be ready. I don't use a gun. Bad medicine."

"I saw a deer today, walking here. It stood and looked at me, then away, then back. I could have shot it . . ." Brian didn't know why he said this, only that it seemed the right thing to do.

"Did it look the way you are going when it looked away?"

Brian thought about it. "Yes. North, up the portage."

Billy nodded. "It was your medicine deer, telling you the right way to go."

"Medicine deer?"

Billy pointed at the sky. "From there. I have a medicine crow that points for me. You have a deer to help you. Always listen to the deer."

"So . . . it's not right to hunt them then?"

"They will tell you when it is right. Listen and they will show you, like today."

Brian nodded and they were silent again for a long time. Brian thought about the grouse and the rabbits he had almost shot. But they hadn't seemed the same. The deer stood out. He realized he was tired. His leg had stiffened a bit – though much less than this morning when he'd started – but he'd paddled against the wind much of the day, then portaged, then hunted. He felt a bit stiff and his belly was full and the fire was warm.

"Time to make sleep," Billy said.

He moved to his canoe and crawled under it. From one of the thwarts he pulled an old blanket, wrapped himself in it and was asleep before Brian could finish setting up his tent. Brian unzipped the opening, pulled his bag in and was sound asleep before his head was all the way down.

SEVENTEEN

Dear Caleb: I found today that you don't always have to do a thing as long as you're ready to do it . . .

Brian awakened gradually. The stiffness in his body from paddling hard all day was gone, replaced with an easy looseness that made him feel almost light.

He unzipped the bag and stepped out of the tent and was surprised to see that Billy was gone. Canoe, old cooking pot, all of it gone and he hadn't heard a thing. Brian moved away from the campsite and relieved himself and came back and saw something tied to the thwart of his canoe. He went closer. It was a short piece of a whitetail deer tail – tan and white hair on a bit of leather – with a crow feather tied next to it and both on a rawhide loop.

It was medicine, he thought. Billy had left it for him. He slipped the loop over his head. His medicine, a deer, and Billy's, the crow feather, hung around his neck. He had two ways to see things now, two ways to know . . .

He would think on Billy later, think on him and how he had come to be, and he would wonder where Billy was going, just as he thought Billy might wonder where Brian was going. But for now it was enough that they had had stew and sat by the fire, and Brian felt himself looking out as he packed the canoe, looking out of himself ahead at the horizon, the sky; not thinking of himself or what he was about but just seeing the world as he moved through it, and that came from Billy, watching Billy's hands as he spoke, listening to the music of his words.

There was no wind and he paddled hard that day. By the map he judged he'd come more than thirty miles, leaving only perhaps sixty-odd miles to Williams Lake.

He caught fish for dinner again that night – this time the bare hook didn't work and he had to get some worms from a rotten log – and had rice and fish. The grouse stew the night before had been delicious but the potatoes seemed heavy in his gut. The rice tasted good.

He set up camp with practiced skill and that night when it rained – not hard or long but enough to make everything wet and new looking – the water ran off the tent and into the ditch and flowed away down to the lake and he slept dry and comfortable. He awakened and listened to the rain on the tent for a time, then went back to sleep and did not awaken again until the sun was on the tent in the morning.

That day he paddled on three short lakes with small creeks between them. At the end of the last lake the creek leading to the next one was so shallow it would not take the canoe with Brian's weight in it so he stepped out barefoot and began to pull the canoe along with just his gear in it, and he was wading along the creek in the late afternoon, when he ran into the bear.

He had seen bear before, had been attacked or at least rolled around by one, and knew that usually they didn't bother people, wanted only to be left alone.

It was a young bear, not terribly big, perhaps two hundred and twenty pounds, and it was alongside the creek when Brian came around a turn, pulling the canoe. It had been rolling logs over along the side of the creek, looking for grubs.

"Woof!" It made a sound exactly like a dog's bark would be written. A clean *woof*, and stood up.

It was a ticklish moment. Brian knew that bear rarely attacked. But he also knew it wasn't particularly good when they stood up and didn't run away, and this bear was standing not ten feet from him.

Brian had left his bow on top of the pack with an

arrow nocked to the string but it was a field point, not a broadhead, and a field point would do almost no damage to a bear, probably just make it angry. By the time he got a broadhead out of the quiver and got a shot the bear would be on him.

He looked down and to the side to avoid eye contact (which sometimes angered them) and – still holding the rope to the canoe so that it angled roughly between them – he slowly backed away.

The bear dropped to all fours and lunged toward him.

Brian jumped off to the left.

The bear stopped, watched, then lunged to its right, Brian's left, heading off Brian's movement in that direction.

Brian moved back to his right, trying to get back across the stream.

The bear lunged out into the water, this time to its left forcing Brian back the other way.

It's pushing me, Brian thought. It's making me go back on the bank. It wants me . . .

The bear feinted again to the right, pushing Brian back, left, then right, the area getting smaller all the time; Brian kept moving back, pulling the canoe, keeping the canoe between them, zigging and zagging, always back, across the shallow stream and close to the bank on the far side.

The bear was teasing him, playing with him,

maybe the way a cat plays with a mouse, back and forth, cutting him off, tightening down on him. Brian felt it rise in him then; he had been afraid, the way the bear was working him, like prey, and that changed to full-blown anger.

"No!"

His voice almost made Brian jump. The bear stopped dead, startled, and stood up again.

"Not with me . . ." Brian took the half beat to reach into the canoe and grab his bow, another half second to get a broadhead out of the quiver, nock it to the string, raise the bow and stand.

They weren't twenty feet apart and now there was eye contact. The bear was close to the same height as Brian and there was no fear in its eyes and there was no fear in Brian's. Just two sets of eyes looking at each other across the top of a razor-sharp MA-3 broadhead.

"Go away." Brian said it quietly but as he spoke he looked down from the bear's eyes to the center of the bear's chest, looked where the heart was beating, looked, and the point of the arrow dropped to where his eyes were looking and he drew the bow halfway back, then full, tucked the arrow under his chin and said again, softly, "Go away now."

There was nothing else for Brian then but the arrow and the bowstring trembling slightly in his fingers and the broadhead that he would send into the bear's heart and the bear standing there, looking at him – no birds singing, no ripple of water past the canoe, no other thing in the world but one man and one bear in a moment perhaps older than time, a bear, a man and quiet death. Had the bear moved toward him again, or snarled, or lunged – any wrong start or any wrong motion – Brian would have released the arrow.

Instead the bear hovered for a time – it seemed forever – and then came to a decision, let air gently from its nose in a long sigh, lowered slowly to all fours, turned and ambled away down the creek bed the way Brian had come, shuffling along through the shallow water without looking back.

Brian tracked it with the arrow and when it was obvious the bear was going to keep going he let the string go slowly forward – his arms were shaking from holding it back so long – and took a breath.

"Good," he said quietly, almost whispering. "It's good . . . my medicine is strong . . ."

And he was half surprised to find that he was thinking the way Billy had spoken, almost in a song, and that as he had thought he had moved his right hand – the left still holding the bow with the arrow nocked – with his words, waving the medicine down from the sky and waving the bear away.

Good medicine.

EIGHTEEN

*Dear Caleb: I am where I belong and I belong
where I am . . .*

If there had still been something of his old life left
in him – and there may have been just a faint part
of it – it left with the bear, left when he looked over
the broadhead at the bear's heart and knew that he
was not afraid because he was as good as the bear,
as quick, as ready to do what he had to do. Because
he knew he could kill the bear, knew he *would* kill
the bear, he didn't have to kill. He was even with
the bear.

Even with the woods.

Even with his life.

He did not put the tent up that night but made a
fire and had plain rice with salt – he didn't even take
fish – and then propped the end of his canoe upside
down a couple of feet up on a limb, spread his bag
beneath it and went to sleep. The mosquitos came
for a short time; then the night cooled so that they
left and he slept soundly.

The next morning he made tea, packed the canoe and worked ten hours on long lakes with two one-mile portages, making – according to the map – just under thirty miles, with thirty or so miles still to go to Williams Lake and the Smallhorns.

That evening he took fish to mix with his rice, again using a bare hook, and read some Shakespeare before it was dark – still *Romeo and Juliet* – having to reread it six or seven times, standing on the lakeshore speaking aloud out over the water before he thought he understood it.

Just before he finished he found himself speaking to an audience. Two otters came along the shore hunting and stopped to listen to him, floating on their backs in the water with their heads raised attentively as he read them a verse, then reread it:

O, mickle is the powerful grace that lies
In plants, herbs, stones, and their true qualities.
For naught so vile that on earth doth live
But to the earth some special good doth give . . .

When he was finished they rolled over and dove and he did not see them again.

"You could have clapped," he called after them. "Or at least told me what *mickle* means . . ."

But they were gone.

Again he slept without the tent, under the canoe. That night it rained softly a bit but the canoe shed the water and he stayed dry and sometime toward morning he heard a noise, a rustling, and it awakened him and when he went back to sleep he dreamed of Billy.

It was a strange dream. Billy was there, in the woods, and he would point to something – a limb on a tree, a deer standing, a duck flying across the moon – and each time he would point at himself and then back to the scene and at the end he pointed at Brian, then at himself, then back at Brian and that was when Brian awakened and sat bolt upright, so suddenly that he hit his head on the inside of the canoe.

For a moment he sat there, wondering why he was awake. It was dark, though clear and well lighted by the moon, and there was a faint glow in the east. Nothing had disturbed the camp to awaken him, and then he remembered Billy and the dream.

It was there. Billy was his medicine. The deer, perhaps, but Billy as well, and it hit him that when he'd met Billy he was meeting himself years from now, an old man who looked carved in wood moving through and with the forest, being of and with the woods, and he decided that it wouldn't be so bad a thing to be.

He arose and made a fire and had tea and a sugar cube and was packed and moving on the lake in the

113

canoe before daylight. There was another series of long lakes and he could easily make Williams Lake and the Smallhorns that day.

He bit deep with the paddle, the canoe jumping ahead with his stroke, the pack tied in, his bow with a broadhead on the string lying in front of him, wearing only shorts except for the medicine hanging around his neck, burned brown now by the sun, one with the canoe and the lake and the morning and the air, and he was an hour across the lake when he realized he was not going to the Smallhorns.

It was a big map. There were many lakes and rivers to see, much more country to be in, and the Smallhorns would still be there later. He would find them when it was time to find them. He would head this way for a time, then perhaps move west with the sun.

Out ahead was the end of the lake, and out ahead of that another lake and out ahead of that the forest and out ahead of that his life . . .

Just waiting for him to find it.

He leaned forward at the waist, slipped the paddle deep into the water and pulled back again, evenly, his arms and shoulders taking the load. The canoe came alive and seemed to leap ahead.

He would follow his medicine.

114

AUTHOR'S NOTE

This is the final book about Brian, though someday I may do a nonfiction book about those parts of my life that were like Brian's.

Once I knew the truth of the woods, which came to me about the time I wrote *Hatchet*, once I knew what happened, I knew I would write this book. It is perhaps even true that I *always* knew I would write this book, in a way before I wrote *Hatchet* or *The Return* or *Winter*.

A thing happens when you have been taken by the bush, by wilderness. Much is made, and rightly so, of the effects of post-traumatic stress disorder on people who have been in combat, and perhaps there is some of that in the effect that living in the wilderness has on a person – if such a thing can be good and not bad – for when a person has once been possessed by the wild it is not possible for him to be truly normal again.

I started hunting and trapping and fishing in the north woods of Minnesota when I was about eleven. Due to the difficult nature of my childhood

I could not be home and spent much of the time – to the detriment of my grades – in the woods with either an old lemonwood bow and half a dozen homemade arrows or a worn old single-shot Remington .22 rifle that fired only half the time and never ejected right (I had to dig the expended cartridge case out with the tip of a pocketknife).

Virtually all that happens to Brian in these books has happened to me at some point or other in my life. I have been in two forced landings in light planes, though not nearly as severe as the crash Brian suffers in *Hatchet* (although that crash is based on a true incident). I have hunted large and small game extensively with a straight bow, have been attacked by moose several times, have had a bear "play" with me as the bear in this book does with Brian (it is a humbling experience to feel like prey), have had a doe jump into my canoe to get away from flies, have eaten what Brian eats, made fires and cooked the way he cooks, worked and slept beneath a canoe the way he does in this book, lived in lean-tos and holes in the ground and found and believe in my "medicine" (similar to Billy's, mine is a crow).

For nearly twelve years I lived completely in the bush. For most of that period if I did not kill it with a bow and arrow or grow it in a garden or pick it in the woods (berries and hazelnuts) I did not eat it. I supported a family off the woods, as perhaps Brian will. We bought only salt and seasonings and clothing. All food and shelter and heat came from the bush or a garden and it must be said that the quality of the food I ate then far surpasses anything I can buy from the store now, either vegetable *or* animal (though I am now a vegetarian) and it was perhaps the healthiest time of my life.

Once you have seen the horizon, have followed it, have lived with nature in all its vicious beauty, it is impossible to come back to "normal" life. Like Brian, I tried. I bought a house in town with a yard and neighbors – because I thought that was the thing to do – and inside a week I was pacing like a panther in a cage, trying to see out, see across the town to the hills, to the trees, to the woods.

I simply could not do it. I went back to a hut in the mountains of New Mexico and though it was a small version of the bush – I had neighbors as close as three miles away and it was only twelve miles to a small town – I could see the trees and the sky and the horizon and for a time it kept me from going insane. But it was still not enough, still only pretend wilderness, and I found myself taking longer trips on a horse, days at a time, until I would hit a fence that stopped me, and in the end it was the same as before: I paced, pulled against the imaginary chain that held me, hated not being able to move toward the horizon . . . So then I discovered sled dogs and ran two Iditarods.

When I developed heart disease after running those two races I had to give up my sled dogs and could not live in northern winters, and that denied the wild to me. I could not go back to the bush as Brian does in this book, though I tried several times, and I'm not certain what would have become of me had I not rediscovered the sea.

The sea saved me, and it continues to save me. I have always loved it, and at times in my life I had small boats and sailed, not on any long trips, just to local areas in California. But I had moved away from the coast and about the time it became evident that the hut in the New Mexico mountains was still too "tame" (if that is the right word) I found the sea again, right where it has always been, bought an old thirty-eight-foot sailboat, which I spent two years restoring, and went out into what is possibly the only big wilderness left – the Pacific Ocean.

I am there now. It is the winter of 1998 and *El Niño* has made it impossible for me to get across the Pacific until spring and so I sit in San Diego, repairing bits on the boat that seem to break simply because they are on a boat.

I have made two trips down to Mexico with the boat – she (boats have lives, souls, and they are feminine) is named Felicity – to see the Sea of Cortez.

118

Last spring I took her from Mexico up the west coast of the United States, up the inside passage to Alaska, and then turned and came down the outside back to San Diego in preparation for going across to Hawaii, then down to the Marshall Islands and from there to Australia.

Unfortunately, as Brian finds on his return to the bush, man may propose, but nature disposes. *El Niño* has intervened and is lashing the ocean between San Diego and Hawaii with storms and wild southwesterly winds that *Felicity* could not possibly buck.

And so I am writing this on a laptop while seagulls fight over garbage up in the Dumpster at the top of the public docks. There is a soft rain coming down – I can hear it pattering on the skylight hatch over my head – and I have Mozart on the tape player while I wait.

Not long. Just until the wind changes. And then I will go again – always, as Brian must always go.

Gary Paulsen
On the sloop *Felicity*
San Diego Bay, February 1998

Gary Paulsen
Hatchet

There was almost no light when he opened his eyes again. The darkness of night was thick and for a moment he began to panic . . . The world came back. He was still in pain, all-over pain . . .

When a thirteen-year-old city boy crash lands into the Canadian wilderness, all he is left with is a hatchet – and the need to survive. From now on he learns everything the hard way . . .

'A heart-stopping story . . . something beyond adventure.'
Publishers Weekly

'A spellbinding winner.'
Kirkus Reviews

A 1988 NEWBERY HONOR BOOK

Gary Paulsen
Hatchet: The Return

'We want you to do it again . . .'

Two years earlier, Brian had been stranded alone in the wilderness for fifty-four days with nothing but a small hatchet. Yet he survived. Now they want him to do it again – to go back into the wilderness so that others can learn the survival techniques that kept him alive. This time he would not be alone. He would have company and equipment. But the violent forces of nature rob Brian of these luxuries, and he finds himself once more isolated and in danger . . .

Gary Paulsen
Hatchet: Winter

I could freeze to death, he thought. Soon.

Brian was thirteen years old when his plane crashed, leaving him
stranded alone in the Canadian wilderness. Somehow he survived
and – as bestselling *Hatchet* tells – he was rescued at the end of
the summer.

But what if Brian hadn't been rescued? What if he had been left to
confront winter – the deadliest enemy of all? Now the thrilling
story continues . . .